By the same author:

Odds & Socks – A Selection of Short Stories

Pick & Mix

A Selection of Short Stories

by

T. L. Cowell

McKnight & Bishop Ltd

ISBN 978-1-905691-42-5

A CIP catalogue record for this book is available from the British Library

First published in 2014 by McKnight & Bishop Ltd.

McKnight & Bishop Ltd.
28 Grifffiths Court, Bowburn, Co. Durham, DH6 5FD
http://www.mcknightbishop.com
info@mcknightbishop.com

This books has been typeset in Garamond and ParmaPetit

Printed and bound in Great Britain by Bonacia Ltd, Peterborough for

Charles "Chas" Dryden

and

Ronald "Ron" Cowell

About the Author

T. L. Cowell lives in deepest, darkest Norfolk, UK, surrounded by a plethora of pets, most of which have long ears and fluffy tails. She fights a multitude of chronic illnesses including fibromyalgia, chronic migraine, and anxiety, on a daily basis. Her head remains in the clouds, whilst her feet are on the ground. And of course, her nose is still in a book (albeit, a different one from the last time she wrote one of these.)

She is hugely grateful to her writing team – T. Morgan Editing, McKnight & Bishop Publishing, and April Sanders for her cover designs.

Her next publication will be the debut novel, *Alpha*, which is due as soon as her illnesses allow.

You can find T. L. Cowell on the web at:

@tlcwrites (Twitter and Instagram)
T. L. Cowell (Facebook)
tlcowellwrites (Tumblr)

and, now, at her nifty website: www.tlcowell.com

About The Publisher

McKnight & Bishop are always on the lookout for great new authors and ideas for exciting new books. If you write or if you have an idea for a book, email us:

info@mcknighbishop.com

Some things we love are: undiscovered authors, open-source software, crowd-funding, Amazon/Kindle, social networking, faith, laughter and new ideas.

Visit us at: **www.mcknightbishop.com**

Contents

Tall Tails

Ah, so you're back, are you?

Back for more stories, back for more everyday magic?

That's good. I like kids with a good sense of imagination. I like kids who are always trying to learn more about the world. I like kids who have, ha, a nose for trouble, shall we say?

Not that I'm trouble, oh no, oh no, no, no, of course I'm not. Hee hee, but that doesn't mean that your parents necessarily want you here, does it? It doesn't mean that they agree with you knocking on the doors of little old ladies and demanding entrance, tea and oho, yes, plenty of cookies.

But then, that would be more than a little hypocritical of them, wouldn't it? Oho, yes, it was them standing where you are now. Them with the scuffed shoes and grass-stained shirts and a little lopsided grin, hoping for a tad more magic in their lives.

Hee hee, they do say these things run in the family, don't they?

Come in, come in. No friends, this time? Just you on your lonesome? Oh no, no, no, that's not necessarily a bad thing. It is rather chilly outside, is it not? Oho, you're the only one willing to brave the pouring rain and the windy gales. That's fine, that's fine. I have a little something to warm your cockles. Ah, but you knew that already, didn't you?

Have a coconut macaroon, if you want. More potassium than a banana, they say. Hee, potassium, it's good for growing bones and inquiring minds. Ah, not so good for people with defunct kidneys, mind. Your aunt ought to watch out for them.

How did I know that? Hee, well, I have eyes and ears everywhere, don't I?

Still, still, take your hot chocolate and a seat. And wipe your nose. Oho, it seems the cold got into you anyway. After all, you're not listening to your parents, being here and all in this weather, aren't you? You can at least listen to my rule whilst you're here.

That's better, much better. Now, where were we? Stories, oh yes, I still have many of them. Oh, do you want to hear more about my precious old photograph, or something new? Or do you just want to wait and see where my mind leads?

Hee hee, yes, it is true. My mind does tend to wander down fine tangents, doesn't it?

No need to be so surprised. Haha, Mister is just looking for his treats. He seems to think you have something for him, can't you see? Oho, it's all in his green eyes. That cat of mine, hee, he sure could tell you a story or two if you gave him half a chance.

You're sceptical? Why? Oh, cats can be far cleverer than you think. Dogs may be considered to be man's best friend, but that doesn't mean that cats can't feel love and affection just as deeply— and, if not, more so—for their human companions.

Why the disbelief? Have I ever steered you wrong? You've come here time after time, sampled many of my wares—I believe that the lavender ice cream, the one that helps you sleep at night, is one of your favourites? And you listen to my stories. Oh, even when there's a whole bundle of you here, you sit front row with your ears and your eyes open. Aha, I mean, I even know that you won't tell a soul where you've been all day. Mister and his fluffy fur might sell you out, though.

There's a power in that. Hee, you know. Everyday magic, that's what it is. I like to think that I, ah, have a way with words, shall we say?

Look, see, Mister has settled down now. Go ahead, give him a stroke, he won't mind. Enjoy the feel of his soft fur between your fingertips. Oho, make sure you scratch him behind the ear, that's his favourite spot.

Cats have a language all their own, you know. They can manipulate things until it is just right for them. Kittens learn it from birth. Oh, yes, you've seen a cat kneading at a blanket until it is perfect, right? You've seen them refuse to settle until everything is just so. It's all manipulation; it's their kind of magic.

Aha, you should never doubt a lady like me. I know cats; I know their ear twitches and the swish of their tails and the way they speak. They have a magic all their own and that's why certain people are attracted to them. It's why others loathe them with the very core of their being.

Honestly, of all the pets that people could possibly keep, cats are the most popular and the most misunderstood at the same time. Hee, people either love them or don't. Me, oho, it is quite obvious on which side of the fence I sit.

I remember, many a moon ago, hearing of a kitten. A small scrap of a thing, it was just a ball of black and white fur. Barely old enough to be separated from her mama, the poor thing. Oh, how my heart breaks just thinking of the state the poor little scrap of fur was in.

You see, the weather was not all that dissimilar to today's. Blustery, wet and wild, with the taste in the air that something worse might be on the horizon. How can a small kitten survive the worst that winter has to throw at her?

Hmm, oh, yes, go ahead, take another macaroon. It's my own special recipe, you know. There's plenty more where that came from. Oh, don't worry about me, my dear, I always make far more than I can manage on my lonesome.

Hee hee, though, of course, Mister likes to try and help himself to more than his fair share. I mean, there are certain things that dear little cats shouldn't be eating. Oho, yes, of course I try to tell him that, but it won't do. He has his own will, his own desires. And yes, Mister likes to explore the world through the sense of taste. It'll be his own undoing one of these days.

Anyway, I digress. Where was I? Oho, yes, the little black and white kitten, homeless and motherless on a damp, dreary, and desolate day. I remember, honestly, I do.

So, then. This kitten, she may have been young but she has already learned a lot. She knows things, she can change her luck at the swish of her tail. It's innate, you know, hee, yes. She was born with certain skills and already had the chance to learn from mama before they were separated.

These skills, they mean she knows who to look for, what to do, how to find the right person. She knows that she can't take care of herself, especially not on a day when her whiskers sensed snow and frost were on the way.

She can tell the sort of home where a kindly person, maybe an old lady or one with young children with big hopeful eyes, will let her stay. They'll feed her and water her, let her sleep on a warm bed or in front of a toasty fire. Oho, and there won't be anything to be afraid of, least of all a dog with a strong aversion to cats.

It's all about reading the lay of the land, you see. Ah, yes, kittens can do that. They are attracted to good people. They know. Hee, you may disbelieve me all you like, you can doubt it with that crease of your eyebrows, but it doesn't mean it's not the truth.

Me, aha, I've seen it too many times in my years to not be able to see some truth between the lines. Everywhere, there's that truth. In people's body language, in the way they cook, in their handwriting, the way they breathe, even. No matter what words they say, there's something giving them away.

And cats, cats know. Hee, they know who they can trust and oh, who would rather drown a bedraggled kitten than save its life. Our kitten, she knew what to look for, and if not, the swish of that tail of hers would tell her otherwise.

It took time, the sun was setting and she most likely traversed, oh maybe a mile or so before getting to the right area. Oho, yes you're right; it wouldn't have been safe for her. She possibly had a close shave with a speeding car or narrowly avoided a fox.

But the house, the house she was looking for, it was right at the end of the street, if I am remembering correctly. The porch light was on and the lounge showed the scene of a family settling down to dinner. Hee, oh, or maybe it was a sweet old lady, with a cup of tea, talking to her friends from the book club. Even a lonely man looking for a young lady to fill in a void in his life.

Whatever the situation, oh, she knew this was the place where she'd be loved. Whomever they were, there was an absence in their life. The memory of a childhood pet, of fluff and fur and claws and purrs. An empty, never-used cat basket in the corner. Some food bowls gathering water by the back door. Oh, yes, once they were used for a familiar friend, but at that moment in time, they were left outside 'for the hedgehogs' and other wildlife.

Hee, but that is of no import. The fact is, that this person—or these people—were missing a cat, even if they didn't know it yet.

Sometimes, a cat will be able to break into a house and make themselves at home before their new companions even realise they have her there. Other times, aha, they will just appear in the garden from time to time before a friendly hand beckons them in on a permanent basis.

But this little kitten? She mewed piteously by the back door. Hee hee, there was an old, locked cat flap there. She was too small, too weak to force it open by then. But the sound, it travels.

Our little black and white kitten, she was one of the lucky ones. She had a home and a family that loved her. There are so many kittens born in the wild that simply won't make it. Ah, it's sad, I know, but people are irresponsible by nature. Hee, oh yes, you and I included. But people, they love their pets, but that's not always enough to do what is right by them.

Ah, but this little girl, I know she was fine. Her new family took her to the vets, made sure she got strong and healthy. She had the operation to stop her from having kittens, and all of her vaccinations. Hee, yes, these owners took proper care of this little girl. Good people, they were.

There was good food here. Scrunchy balls to play with, maybe even fish in a huge tank that she would be able to sit and watch on a daily basis.

Oho, like I said, she's one of the lucky ones.

What about the others, her littermates and ones like her? Is that what you said? You shouldn't speak with your mouth full. Ha, yes, that's why. Your food could end up in your lap.

The others, yes, they weren't so lucky. Maybe they didn't learn off of their mama properly and stayed trapped in a dangerous situation, with people who don't love them right. Maybe they were taught to survive on their wits and, oh yes, never learn the joys of a loving human. Ah, it's a problem to be sure. You know that, you're a clever one.

And, oho, yes, sad to say, but there's always more just like this poor wee litter on their way into the world.

Ah, but let's just focus on the lucky ones for today. I'm an old dear; I can't be dealing with doom and gloom. Hee, let's take Mister, here. I rescued him. Found him at the end of the garden, with fur matted, and he was shivering. He knew I'd be here for him; he was merely waiting for me to find him. Yes, I'm talking about you, Mister, now go back to sleep. This story hasn't been *about* you.

Animals know, but cats especially. They know where they are safe, and they know where they are loved. All they ever look for is that mutual respect. They have survival skills, one way or another.

You do respect animals, do you not?

Good, that's good to hear. Yes, yes, I think you're a good egg. And, hee hee, I think Mister agrees with me too.

But look at the time! It's already dark; it's getting late. Best you go back home, have some dinner and go to bed.

Just remember to keep your eyes and ears open. You never know who is looking for you, do you? Oho, yes, I do have an inkling that maybe something—someone—special is waiting for you just around the corner.

It could be your new best friend, albeit one of the four-legged variety. Just make sure you respect her and she'll feel the same. Then there will be safety, security, and most importantly, love.

And what can be more magical than that?

Chance

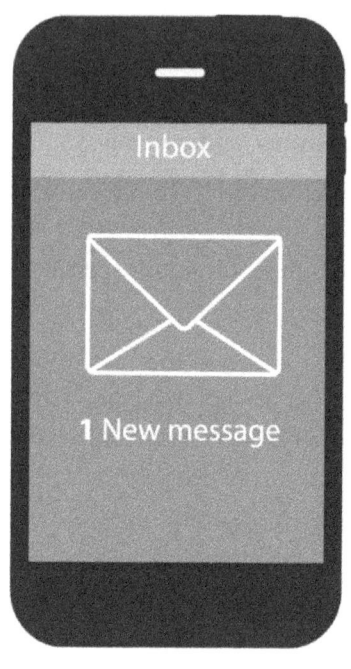

You have used up your last chance. Life will be terminated shortly. Thank you for using the Chanceometer and goodbye.

"But I've done nothing wrong. What happened, I don't deserve to—"

The querulous, panicked words were cut off with a scream. He fell to the ground, stone dead, and then deathly silence enveloped the busy marketplace. Nobody moved until a small girl with long blond hair reaching her waist and shaking hands, pushed through the gobsmacked crowds.

"Heidi, no," somebody called. The woman's voice sounded almost as scared as the dead man's had been prior to his passing. "You shouldn't touch them. You need to call for the auditors, you know this."

Heidi ignored her mother, pushed her long hair behind her ear and knelt down beside him. Glassy brown eyes gazed lifelessly back at her. Slowly, Heidi reached forward and with small hands, she closed them. "There," she declared. "It looks like he is sleeping now."

Despite the protestations of her mother, she plucked the phone out of his dead hands and read the message. She was a bright, curious girl. Her mother repeatedly told her that *curiosity killed the cat*, but she had to know why.

The Chanceometer never told you why you lost chances, though. It only told you that your chances of remaining alive were being whittled away to nothingness. This man wasn't old. Heidi could only wonder how and why he had lost all of his chances so quickly.

Heidi's phone bleeped at her. She had owned it for as long as she could remember. Once, she had asked her mother if she'd actually been born with it in her hands. Her mum had just tousled her hair and smiled at what a little silly her daughter could be. Her father had told her to stop asking such stupid questions.

He'd died shortly after. Mum had never bothered to explain how or why. Heidi couldn't help but wonder if all of his chances had run out. If he'd caught something too fine, done something a little too risky, or simply really, really upset somebody.

She shivered, dropped the dead man's phone and picked up her own.

You have used up one chance. You have ninety-eight remaining. Please spend your life wisely. Thank you and goodbye.

"Mum..." Heidi started. The phone was blank again. It wasn't like a real phone, not really. You couldn't call anyone up or send a text message or anything. Still, because it was the same size and shape as a mobile phone, everyone just called it their second phone. Or their life phone. Or their chance phone. Mostly, it was referred to as the phone. "Mum, why have I lost a chance?"

Heidi's mother raked her fingers through her wispy greying hair. "I told you, Heidi, I told you to listen to me. The auditors, they don't like it if you mess with their property."

"But he wasn't somebody's property! He was a man!"

"He's dead. He's none of your concern," her mother answered abruptly and dragged Heidi away from the man, through the gaping crowd. Heidi's ear hurt. It was the only piece of her flesh her mum had been able to grab hold of.

"But he died, right there, in front of me. He looked fine and then he was dead. There has to be a reason. Why would he die like that?"

"Stop asking questions, Heidi." Her mother peered around, looking fearfully from left to right.

Words her father had once told her, one of the few things Heidi could remember about him, sprang to mind: *there are eyes and ears everywhere, Heidi Bear. Be careful. You never know who might be listening in. You never know how many chances it could cost you.*

She knew that some things cost more chances than others. She'd seen the news; two dead bodies together. One body was bloodied and beaten, the other looking completely untouched. Not a suicide pact, but a murder and somebody relinquishing all of their chances as a consequence.

But this man, he hadn't looked evil or wrong or like he'd even been really bad at all. He looked like a normal man. Somebody who was like her dead dad maybe, or her mum, or her teachers, or the doctor, or anyone, really. How could he have used up his last chance like that? How could he have used them all up? What did he do wrong? Why did he die?

"But Mum, you know there's something... something not right about what happened to that man. What's going on? Why do we even have the phones anyway?"

"Heidi, I said be quiet!"

Almost simultaneously, both of their phones beeped. Without even having to look, Heidi knew they had both lost a chance. She had never lost two chances in a day before.

In fact, she had only lost one chance, once before. And that was because she had accidentally kicked a boy in the face during kickboxing class. Really, that wasn't her fault at all. After all, they were training. It was to be expected.

But claiming chances back was apparently impossible. Her mum had pleaded and cajoled with somebody on the phone, the house phone, the phone that can actually make calls, for hours on end. All that happened was that she ended up losing a chance for 'wasting an auditor's time.' Heidi wasn't meant to know that happened; she had overheard as her mother mouthed off in disgust outside her bedroom at night.

At the time, Heidi had been half-surprised that her mum hadn't lost a chance for that as well.

Still, this simultaneous loss of chances between them was enough to keep her cowed. She shrank back from her mother, hanging her head in shame. Heidi's long blond hair blew into her face, with no thanks to the wind, and she did nothing to sort it out.

Her mother, meanwhile, didn't bother to check her phone either. Instead, she reached out for Heidi and enveloped her into a bone-crushing hug. "I love you, Heidi Bear. I love you, baby girl. I love you, I love you. I need you, Bear, please let's not argue, let's just get home. I love you."

The world had never seemed like a kind place to Heidi. She had been a quiet person, she kept to herself. Even at kickboxing class she was studious and polite. She never tried to push the boundaries. That was why, at eleven, she still had so many chances left. Most of the people at school, she knew, had lost chances for stupid things. They answered teachers back or lashed out as youngsters, or even were squalling babies who drove their parents to distraction. It was strange, what dictated bad behaviour and what didn't. There was no consistency.

Her whole perception had been altered by what she had just witnessed. Her mother clutched Heidi to her bosom, but all Heidi could see was flashbacks of that man. One minute, alive and well, the next crashing to the floor like a ragdoll. It didn't seem right. It didn't seem fair.

Why, why did they live determined by their phones? Not the calling phones, the chance phones. Why did everyone have one from birth and why did it dictate when and where somebody should die?

People had to learn by their mistakes, didn't they? The Chanceometer didn't give people that long to actually learn. There were always new mistakes being made, new lessons that people had to take into account. Nobody got absolutely everything completely right the first time. Not unless they were some sort of fictional hero or something like that.

Some people, some boys especially it seemed, never managed to keep hold of chances for long. They always ended up boasting about how many chances they had left. They called it pushing the boundaries, Russian Roulette, playing against the odds, rolling the die. The fewer chances they had left, the cooler they apparently were.

Maybe, just maybe, their parents were the cautious sorts. Maybe they hadn't seen a man die before their very eyes. Maybe they hadn't heard him begging the chance phone for another *chance* with his very last breath. Perhaps they thought it was just a rumour and speculation, a game. Perhaps they didn't realise that running out of chances literally meant death.

Who had come up with this system and why was it considered so important? Whose great idea was it to sort out society by enforcing the phones, with the inbuilt Chanceometer? It seemed so morbid, so sick. Why would one person have the divine right to dictate when people had been too dangerous and needed wiping out? Heidi could understand certain aspects, like murderers, but why normal people who liked to live life on the edge?

Besides, it was like a dictatorship. Everyone had to live by the black-and-white rules set out by the Chanceometer. Somebody had had to sit down and consider what was right and what was wrong. And that was the bias. What was good behaviour to one person was surely bad behaviour to another. It was stupid and unfair. It was mass cleansing of society dictated upon when somebody had failed to toe the line for the hundredth time. Who had the right to decide when that was?

And yet, somebody did seem to have that right. After all, it was a fact of everyday life that people had their phones.

Heidi had heard rumours of people losing chances for leaving their phones at home so it couldn't monitor their behaviour, or something stupid like that. That struck Heidi as incredibly unfair. Kids were still learning about what was important and what wasn't. Adults, meanwhile, could simply be forgetful. You couldn't be expected to remember to have something with you all of the time, could you?

But still, people didn't complain about it. At least, they didn't complain about it in public, not when there were apparently eyes and ears everywhere. The only time Heidi had heard somebody speak up was today, when that man had used up that final chance and started begging an inanimate object not to kill him.

How had society come to a place where they needed observing and monitoring to such a degree? And why did nobody speak up? Why was everybody so quiet and accepting of the phones?

Why, now, was she finally beginning to question the role they played? It was something that she should have started thinking about ages ago. Instead, like a sheep, she had followed the crowd and accepted her phone as a part of day-to-day life. Heidi felt like she had been brainwashed into believing that this device was okay.

Witnessing a death because of the phone had opened up a figurative can of worms in her brain.

After all, there were instances when things were dubious, morally grey. What about somebody speeding in their car, something considered bad behaviour, but only because they were rushing their wife to the hospital in order for her to give birth to their baby? What about somebody begging for food because they were starving and had nowhere else to turn? Or what if somebody had to kill a pet dog, but only because it was about to kill a child?

The phones didn't discern between these behaviours which were for the greater good, even if it wasn't something they should be doing. It couldn't even seem to tell the difference between accidents and behaviour which people had chosen to do.

Heidi remembered losing that first chance, that one at kickboxing. She had apologised profusely to the boy, his parents, her sensei, the whole class. She had practiced a roundhouse kick and the boy had walked into the path of her kick. Still, Heidi had felt incredibly guilty and lost a chance because of it. She hadn't even meant to do it.

As Heidi clung tightly onto her mother, she thought about it all. The situation was so incredibly unjust. Their lives were tied to a piece of technology and it was never meant to be that way. Humans were meant to be free to live, to learn from their mistakes and move on.

Ten long years passed. Heidi, at every moment, made sure she preserved her chances as much as feasibly possible. She lived in fear of dying unnecessarily, like her father, and her mother after.

Her mum had died two years ago. She remembered the last words clearly: *I'm sorry.* Heidi didn't know how her mother had whittled down her chances so quickly, but the Chanceometer had decided it was time for her to die.

Clinging onto the pendant, a St Christopher, which hung around her neck, Heidi tried to shake away these thoughts of anger and bitterness. She wanted retribution; she wanted society to be fair again.

As far as she was concerned, the human race had stalled in their development. People were too scared to push the boundaries and figure out new things. Everybody was stuck in their little boxes, living as best they could. They felt like they had to stick to the rules, or they would burn fast and die young.

Despite appearances, Heidi didn't hold much stock when it came to her life. What was the point in living if you weren't *really* living at all?

After all, she was tied to the phone and the Chanceometer within. It changed life from an adventure to mere existence. People were born, they lived, and they died. The Chanceometer made everything so bland and meaningless. There was no spice, no excitement.

This wasn't a life at all.

And people, they had moulded to the ideals of the Chanceometer. Instead of fighting the system, they accepted it and believed it to be justice. Instead, it was a prison cell with no bars. Innocent and guilty alike, everyone was jailed.

Heidi wasn't going to live like that. Not anymore.

She hadn't been cautious, hadn't been trying to save her chances for no apparent reason.

No, she had been keeping her head down and trying to remain invisible for a purpose. She was going to bust open the whole system and give the world their lives back.

Or at least, that was the intention.

She had found like-minded people. Usually, they were the ones who had seen too many people die too young, all because they had thrown caution to the wind a few too many times. They were scarred by their losses, bitter and disillusioned by a system that allegedly protected society.

But, when the government seemed to make increasingly sketchy decisions about the country as a whole, how was it that they were being protected at all? On the contrary, it felt like the little people were on a choke chain whilst the heads of state got to run riot and ruin the world.

If the politicians could have such freedom and get away with it, why, then, couldn't people like her be trusted to make the same kind of judgments? The only reason politicians got away with what they were doing was because they weren't threatened by those they were meant to represent. Nobody could disagree with them and make their sentiment heard, for fear of losing a chance.

Humans had figuratively had their teeth taken out. They had been cowed into silencing their bark. Ten years since she had witnessed that man dying, Heidi had watched as her fellow countrymen had turned into kicked dogs, or trained parrots. Or both, at the same time; that seemed far more accurate. It was stupid and unfair.

So, she had sought out these like-minded people. Whilst being careful not to break the supposed rules, she learned everything that they knew.

It wasn't easy. Words, though often ridiculed as being nothing but wind, were actually powerful. Words could inspire loyalty. Words could inspire hope. Words could spread truth and lies. Words could inspire rebellions. Words could invoke fear. How often had a simple message from the Chanceometer led to terror in the eyes of the reader?

Sometimes it was hard to judge if words would be enough to trigger the Chanceometer. Was spreading dissent and questioning the very fabric of society enough to lose a chance? Or was it just action? If anything, Heidi knew that it was getting tougher to do everything exactly in accordance with what the Chanceometer and those who ran it wanted.

She knew because she was now one of those to lay down the proverbial law.

It was an intentional choice, of course. Heidi wanted to fight the enemy from within. That seemed like the most sensible course of action. It was the journey she had decided upon in the days, weeks, and months after she had witnessed that man die when she was twelve years old. She could still remember the smell of her mother's hair as they hugged, after simultaneously losing chances over some stupid argument.

Now, though, Heidi knew she was about to lose a heck of a lot of chances.

But it didn't matter. Some things were worth dying for.

Besides, trying to manipulate the system from within was too slow. When she had been hired, the colleagues thought she was a bright spark, a model citizen and the ideal young woman to help represent the choices made by the Chanceometer.

As time rumbled on, though, her colleagues had grown suspicious. Heidi challenged their opinions sometimes, tried to make them question their decisions and behaviours. But they were in it too deep. They believed in the Chanceometer where she did not. Instead of the perfect young woman, they saw somebody who talked too much about the wrong things.

It seemed, now, she was going to have to change the world with her own hands.

Cowards. That was what everybody around her was. The secret group she had formed, none of them had stood beside her. Theoretically, they wanted to rid everybody of the phones and the damned Chanceometer. They wanted it to be replaced with appropriate punishment for appropriate crimes, rather than the arbitrary loss of chances that culminated in a loss of life. They all agreed it was unfair, unjust, inhumane.

But not one of them was willing to take action. A few had tried to change things from the inside, like Heidi had. One or two worked in different departments for the Chanceometer, but not close enough for them to talk when on the job.

However, even they, who knew just how frustrating and slow the process of working for the sheep that ran the Chanceometer was, they did nothing. They weren't willing to put their lives on the line and stand up for what they truly believed in.

Heidi was. She reached out for her St Christopher pendant again and allowed her fingers to brush along the gold. Whispering a prayer to a God she wasn't sure she believed in, she reached into her bag for the wire cutters and began to snip.

The phone in her murky brown rucksack bleeped. Heidi didn't bother to look. She knew it was the Chanceometer, telling her that she had broken the rules and lost a chance. The question was, just how much was criminal damage to a wire fence worth? She shook her head. She had to try and get in as far as possible.

She knew the building inside out and upside down. It was ludicrous that the whole system was built in one building and controlled all of society from within it. Surely they should have learned from past mistakes and put a back-up system in place?

Heidi distinctly remembered a time when this building had suffered a major power cut for twenty-four hours. She recalled the insanity and the desperate fervour of the staff trying to get everything back up and running smoothly as quickly as possible.

She witnessed first-hand the reaction of society freed from the claws of the device.

Some went mad. They committed all the crimes they had dreamed of doing but had no gumption to carry out when controlled by the devices. In the centre of cities, it was mayhem with graffiti springing up on walls, windows broken and fist fights occurring in car parks. One murder was committed and the criminal was never caught. People had put all their reliance in the Chanceometer and it failed them.

However, the vast majority of people just went about day-to-day life as if nothing had changed. They were aware of what was going on; the news channels broadcasted the crimes into living rooms across the nation. But they didn't want to break the rules. They had the chance to commit all sorts of heinous acts but were more than willing to act as civilised human beings.

That gave Heidi the faith she needed to believe she was absolutely behaving in the correct manner.

She slipped through the hole she had made in the fencing. The sharp ends of the wires caught on her rucksack and mud slicked up on her clothes. The phone, yet again, messaged her. Once more, Heidi ignored it. She knew it was punishing her for breaking and entering into the building.

Theoretically, she needn't have risked losing chances this way. She could have just done it on a typical work day, one where she had the right to be inside. However, with all the staff surrounding her on all sides, Heidi knew she would never have had a chance to carry out the crimes she wanted to commit.

Once upon a time, there had been a loophole. People could simply 'forget' their Chanceometer, commit all the crimes they wanted, and lose just the one chance due to absent-mindedness. Of course, that loophole had long since been closed after the chaos that had ensued as news got around. Now, if people dared leave the house without their Chanceometer, they would feel excruciating pain, like a migraine, but ten times worse. The pain only increased as they got further from their Chanceometer, but dissipated as they grew closer to it once more. People had literally been driven insane by separation from their Chanceometers. Going without it simply wasn't an option.

But, in the dead of the night, without a star in sight and the smell of petrichor heavy in the air, this was the best chance she had. After all, there was only a skeleton crew manning the whole site at night, people who slept by day and worked by night. These were security guards and basic technicians, individuals who could solve minor issues, should they arise.

They would never really be equipped to deal with somebody so focused on their task, especially not with the whole level of criminal intent that she had. It wasn't criminality, not to Heidi, even if the Chanceometer disagreed. No, it was saving the world. She was saving people from themselves, and freeing them from the shackles that bound them. At least, that was what Heidi repeated to herself as she darted across the damp grass to the imposing grey building that was her workplace.

As her hand pressed against the metal door, the phone bleeped again. As she padded through the hallways, trying desperately to avoid the line of security cameras, the noise became increasingly persistent. Heidi tried to blank it out; she couldn't worry about all the chances she was losing. She knew this would happen.

What she had to do was get to the centre of the building, to the central operations room and the control computer. She had to get there before she ran out of chances, otherwise she would end up throwing her life away for nothing.

She turned a corner and spotted Dave, one of the night security men prowling the hallway, the light of his torch catching dust motes in the air.

Heidi closed her eyes, tried to slow her breathing and prayed that he hadn't spotted her.

"Heidi? What are you doing here?"

Cursing her bad luck, Heidi rounded on him in a rage. She had stuck to her kickboxing, even after losing that one chance. Eventually, Heidi had become a black belt and remained steadfast to her training.

It was ironic, really. They were allowed to study martial arts, but had no real use for them. For some reason, there was an argument that it taught honour and respect. Some individuals said that it was useful to study for defensive purposes, but what was the use when violence was scarce? People prided themselves on the physical aspect of the sport rather than the potential for violence.

Martial arts harked back to the time before the Chanceometer existed, and it was always fiercely contested whether they should be allowed to continue at all. Ruefully, Heidi was glad that, thus far, they had been allowed to continue, in part due to the historical importance, but mostly to encourage exercise in people who might have ordinarily languished in front of televisions or the like all day.

Her oaths and promises to her sensei meant nothing now. The judgment of the Chanceometer meant nothing now. With a swift roundhouse kick to the head, Dave was lying prone on the floor. He had fallen hard; there was a small cut seeping blood near his right ear. Ordinarily, she would have stopped to help, but she didn't have time.

After all, her crimes were ascending as her chances descended. Time was of the essence. It felt like her heart was going to give out before her chances did, though. It was going at ten to the dozen and Heidi could hear it thrumming away in her ears.

As she got closer to the central operations room, she could hear the sound of footsteps in other hallways. She knew that the skeleton crew was now one member down as Dave was unconscious by her doing. Still, the chances were going down. Before tonight, her chance count had been in the nineties. She had been frugal, beforehand, and had always known she needed to be. She had behaved impeccably and as carefully as possible when it came to toeing the line.

How many chances did she have left now? Thirty? Twenty? Just ten? Heidi hadn't counted. She hadn't even been able to.

All she had was one task in mind.

The central operations room was unguarded. Heidi didn't waste time trying to pick the lock; she kicked the pine door down instead.

Wincing as she fell through, into the room and onto the ground, it took all of her effort to get back on her feet. Heidi felt like she had broken an arm, but that wasn't going to stop her. Not now. She had to stop people from dying for falling out of love with their spouse or taking the day off work because their child was ill. All these pointless, arbitrary deaths because people had allegedly done things wrong one hundred times.

What was right and what was wrong, anyway? How could life itself be as clear cut as that?

"Heidi," somebody called as she dug the hammer out of her bag. She ignored them and poised the tool directly over the computer. "Don't do it. It doesn't have to come to this."

"Yes, it does."

The hammer fell.

Parley

The sound of hooves clip-clopping forward echoed down the beaten pathway. Alfreida stilled, listening with pin-pricked ears. Slowly, she reached back to her quiver for an arrow. She exhaled, notching the arrow as she trained her eyes through the sight. The action was smooth, fluid. She had been trained to do this since birth.

Alfreida was learning. The Elder had advised her to cool her temper. Her colours were muted. Nobody could see her unless they were actively looking for her. Even so, her forest was still fraught with danger. Too many changes had occurred around here lately. It wouldn't do to flash her colours and make a scene.

She had to protect herself, and the few Elfkin that

remained. Too many had been destroyed by Homo sapiens lately. Too many had died a needless death. Too few were willing to take up arms and fight for what they deserved. Every species, Elfkin included, had the right to live undisturbed, in peace, as they had for generation after generation. Too many of her kind had scurried away, like frightened little dormice, who were scared of their own shadows.

It rankled her. Elfkin were small, and they may have appeared to be inconsequential in the great scheme of things, but one thing they never were was timid. Her kin were denying their birthright, claiming it was simply so they could survive. However, they could have been out there and actually fighting for it instead. The forest wouldn't grow safer if they remained hidden in shadows.

The hoof beats grew nearer. Slowly, surely, Alfreida drew back the bowstring until it was taut.

"Stay your arrow, Elf," announced a commanding voice.

Alfreida jolted and the arrow flew into the air. A poor shot by anyone's standards. She wouldn't be seeing that arrow again.

Her colours flashed, annoyed. Alfreida stepped out of the shadows and looked upwards. A palomino body, blonde swishing tail, and where the neck of the horse should be was the torso of a Homo sapiens. The human body was modestly covered in a net of ivy, twisting up around the milky white flesh and into the long blonde hair. A pointed nose and startlingly blue eyes glared back down at her. A centaur.

"You could see me?" Alfreida answered. She was still annoyed about losing one of her precious arrows.

"If you insist upon flashing your colours so brightly, of course I can see you. It makes you rather difficult to *miss*." The centaur had a haughty tone. It was only natural; they were all snobs, each and every one of them. Alfreida had never met a centaur who could treat another intelligent species with respect.

Alfreida's eyes flashed blood red. She spat down on the rotted leaves, a globule of salvia trickling into the undergrowth. She was miniscule compared to this centaur, but that didn't mean she couldn't stand her ground. Centaurs had their heads in the stars, anyway. They rarely seemed to care what was happening closer to Earth.

Turning away from the centaur, she rested her hand against the trunk of the tree. "It's called *passion*. I shouldn't think you would understand."

"Is this how your precious Elder taught you to talk to your superiors?"

"How can I respect somebody when they have yet to introduce themselves by name?"

Turning her back to the centaur meant two things: Alfreida didn't see her as an enemy, nor did she deign this palomino pony the honour of looking her in the eye. Centaurs were meant to have a brain rattling around between their ears. If they were aware of the other species in the forest and their customs, then that meant she should understand too.

"Divinia," the centaur spoke abruptly. When Alfreida turned, she saw the woman flick her ivy-woven blonde hair back over her shoulder. "And you are Alfreida, are you not, Elf?"

"If you know my name, then you should at least have the decency to use it, Mule."

Divinia nodded slowly. "Touché... Alfreida."

Alfreida felt her spine tingling. She didn't like dealing with centaurs. They were only marginally better than Homo sapiens. Elfkin considered centaurs to be dim-witted and convinced of their own superiority. Just like the Homo sapiens who seemed intent on wreaking havoc and tearing up the natural order of the world. At least, she surmised, centaurs had no wish for wanton destruction.

Divinia swished her tail and pawed at the ground. She was impatient for a response. Probably because she wanted to bury her head in the clouds and decide that scents or stars or the fall of leaves meant something significant was about to happen. Alfreida didn't need to read the supposed signs. She knew something significant was already happening. She had seen the Homo sapiens with unfamiliar colours with her own eyes. She had reported it to the Elder. She had taken it upon herself to make things right.

Still, it was a necessary evil. Alfreida knew this was a battle she couldn't fight on her own. Although she had drawn her bow and arrow on Divinia's approach, that didn't mean she had the intention to shoot. It always paid to be wary, especially when foes were hiding around each and every corner.

The silence stretched on endlessly. Alfreida stared Divinia down. She refused to break first, it wasn't in her nature. Then again, the Elder always said defiance was in her nature. Her skin took on a purplish hue as she recalled his words. *Earth Shaker.*

Somebody needed to do some earth shaking if they were going to fix this mess. The Elder, hunched over in his wigwam, was meant to be wise. Sitting around, doing nothing, and waiting to see what happened was getting them nowhere. That was the kind of attitude centaurs had. She had no reason to believe that Divinia would be any different.

"Feeling better now?" the centaur asked. Her tone was patronising. Alfreida felt smaller than she actually was; maybe she had been acting like a babe in swaddling clothes.

After all, she couldn't afford to push away potential allies. For a centaur, Divinia seemed surprisingly patient with a supposed lesser creature. Many of her kin would have wandered away with a disdainful sigh by now.

Alfreida exhaled slowly, pondering her situation. She couldn't afford to act like a babe, not anymore. Whilst she was young, yes, she was the only one of her kin who seemed content to fight. She tucked flyaway strands of dark hair behind her ears and nodded.

"Good," Divinia replied, satisfied. "I knew you would come to me."

"Don't tell me, it was 'written in the stars,' yes?" Alfreida said, gritting her teeth. Old habits die hard, or so it seemed. No matter how many times she tried to tell herself to grow up a little, she couldn't help but fall back on tried and tested formulae.

"The arts of my species have been passed from generation to generation for millennia. If you do not wish to hear the insight of my kin, then I shall leave." Divinia made to turn away. Alfreida found herself having to avoid hooves, desperately skirting aside and around the gnarled tree trunk. She panted, breathless. It was a close call; she'd nearly been seriously injured by the centaur. "My abilities have been honed, much like yours with the bow and arrow."

"Centaurs used to have a similar skill with these weapons."

"We chose peaceful protest." The words were simple, but nonsensical to Alfeida's pointed ears. "Peaceful protest," she repeated, as if she were talking to some brainless young. "Our minds."

Alfreida snorted. "I should have shot you when I had the chance."

"Your small arrows would cause but a flesh wound in an individual such as I."

"The tips are poisoned," Alfreida retorted.

"Centaurs are skilled in the healing arts, not merely the art of divination."

Alfreida bit on her tongue to stop herself from laughing. For all of Divinia's claims of the intelligence of centaurs, they certainly lacked in imagination. It didn't take a genius to work out where Divinia's parents got inspiration when naming their young.

"Elf, you need to stop insulting me if you wish to hear my insights. You want to change the world around you, but cannot see past the tip of your nose."

Alfreida shrank back. The conversation was somewhat similar to the one she had shared with the Elder. Where he had riled her up, the centaur was shaming her.

But, Divinia was right. If she wanted to make a difference, to change the world, then she had to put old prejudices aside. The unease between their kinds was age-old, but when it came to the Homo sapiens issue, they were on the same side. Alfreida knew that, and she hoped that Divinia did too.

"I..." Alfreida started. She hoisted the bow over her shoulder, readjusted the quiver and threw her shoulders back. Earth Shaker needn't be a bad thing. Earth Shakers could reassert normalcy in the face of danger. But they also needed help. Her task was to seek out the other kin plagued by Homo sapiens. She had found Divinia, or rather, Divinia had found her. Alfreida couldn't throw it away at the first hurdle. "I apologise. Your kin are so different to mine."

"Duly noted." Divinia breathed heavily through her nose, snorting into the cool autumnal breeze. Alfreida watched as brown and orange leaves fell around them, carpeting the established pathways in between the trees. This peace, this quiet, it wasn't going to last forever. One small elf couldn't change everything by herself, but she could put everything into motion. Divinia, she hoped, would be the next step.

"So," Alfreida started.

"I am aware of the unfamiliar Homo sapiens. Their colours are wrong."

"Where did they come from?"

The centaurs should know the answer. After all, they spent their time with their heads in the clouds for exactly this reason. Elfkin were meant to be all about action, but the latest attacks from Homo sapiens had sent them scurrying.

Many deaths had been endured, and her clan had scattered far and wide. Alfreida didn't know if there was even any chance of reunion within the forest.

Regardless, Elfkin simply didn't spend their time looking for what caused things. They were the fixers, the responders, they fought first then thought later. Except for the Elder, of course. His job was to guide his clan through their lives in the forest in the most appropriate way. However, being brought up as an Elf, fighting his way through the clans to the top meant that he still didn't have the kind of perspective to figure out these strange Homo sapiens.

Suddenly, Alfreida was very glad that the first alternative species she had found was a centaur. Fairies were tricksy and had a different opinion on something every other minute, Gnomes cared more about the actual plants than things with lungs, and Dwarves were more interested in what was underneath the surface. Getting all these species on the same page was going to be harder than she initially thought.

The forest felt a lot more crowded. Since seeing the foreign Homo sapiens, Divinia was the first non-humanoid Alfreida had come across. Even so, she was acutely aware that others could be hiding around any tree, any mound of leaves, or hiding amongst the shedding twigs of the canopy.

"There is a war coming. It is written in the—"

"Stars, tea leaves, fires, the ripples of water in the brook," Alfreida interrupted. "There is always one war or another on its way when it comes to you centaurs. I need to know about the here and now."

The centaur shook her blonde hair and ivy mane and stared down at Alfreida with contempt. Divinia was quick to be offended, but at least she hadn't cantered off in a huff. Still, Alfreida needed her to hurry up and get to the point. If there was a war coming, then she wanted to be prepared instead of listening to the supposed wisdom of the centaur for months on end.

"I focus on the wider picture. Only then can I garner enough information to ascertain the patterns in which the world is moving."

"But you knew about those unfamiliar Homo sapiens, you know their colours are wrong." Alfreida started grinding her teeth, and fiddling with her bowstring as she did so. Her own colours were flashing again and she knew the centaur would have noticed that by now. "You must have some opinion on them. Are they going to start this war, or has it already begun? Will they make it worse? Why don't you have any straight answers for me?"

"Cool your temper, Earth Shaker. You need to find these children. They are mere babes, lost in the woods. They need your help to find their way."

"Why couldn't you have said that in the first place?"

"Only then can you ascertain what will happen in the future. They may be friend or foe to the inhabitants of this world."

Alfreida knew she was unlikely to get any more sense out of Divinia. It was this reason she hated talking to centaurs. Generally speaking, they were far too vague for her liking. Would it have really hurt them to be more specific?

Differences. That was what caused tension and war. They needed to learn and understand one another. Fairies, Goblins, Elves, Gnomes, Centaurs and all the others alike.

Maybe even a Homo sapiens or two; they, too, were meant to be a *sapient* species. Talking, trying to understand other viewpoints instead of trampling over them. That was what they all needed to do.

It was a lesson that Alfreida knew she had to learn. Funny, really, that she was the one that came to that conclusion too.

"Can I at least count on you and your kin to meet at the Wishing Tree? Three nights hence?"

"Why?" Divinia's startlingly blue eyes blinked down at her. Alfreida threw back her shoulders, her ebony hair rippling down her back. At least the centaur was curious.

"To talk," Alfreida declared.

She didn't wait for an answer. Instead, Alfreida scooped up her belongings. There was more work to be done.

Finding these strangely coloured Homo sapiens could wait until later. She needed to hear the opinions of other kinds first.

Darker Days Are Coming

Her body was slicked with sweat. She bent over and panted. Once she'd recovered, she glanced up into blinding sunlight and stared bitterly at the horizon. The closer she got to her destination, the further away it felt. Every footstep led to a shooting pain running up her leg. Karen cringed, blinked, and swallowed it all down.

As far as Karen was concerned, this was some kind of personal torture, albeit one that was entirely necessary. Others may not have agreed with her, but she wasn't looking for their approval. The only person whose opinion mattered was her own. The rest of the world was completely irrelevant. It was what she saw in the mirror that needed to be changed.

Karen knew that the search for perfection was a long and arduous journey. Half-hearted measures would never get her anywhere. If she wanted to be the very best, the woman that everybody wanted to be, or to be with, then she had to push herself beyond her very limits.

That was what she had been doing for months now. Her New Year's Resolution was to become the perfect woman and every spare second was spent working towards it. Of course, she wasn't getting very far. The look in the mirror never seemed to be any different.

It teased her. It mocked her. It taunted her.

Every single day was like a battle of wills between herself and the reflection. Some days, Karen didn't even want to bother getting up at all. What was the point when perfection was a fool's errand?

But lazing around and pretending the world didn't exist didn't do anything. Instead, she forced herself to work for what she wanted. Nobody else could do it for her. The look in the mirror may have made her stomach turn, but that didn't mean things couldn't be different one day.

And ultimately, that was why she was out here, running. It was why she had been out here for hours. It was why she had been going for so long that she had lost track of time.

On a more positive note, she decided, that at least meant she had managed to stack up the miles on this late summer's day.

She pushed strands of platinum blond hair out of her eyes. It wasn't natural, of course; she wasn't lucky enough to have been born with beautiful, luscious pale locks. At least it was thick. Although, sometimes she wondered if it was maybe a little *too* thick. Karen let out a puff of irritated air. She had stopped for too long. It was time to move on.

Her family would be waiting dutifully back at home. Dad and Pa. She loved them both until her bones ached and her head spun. She would walk to the end of the earth and back again for them. They would be getting worried now. After all, the sun was setting, it was right in her eyes and she had been out virtually all day.

Pa especially worried about his little girl. Though, these days, she felt like she wasn't quite so little at all. The mirror, as always, never lied. It was callously cruel and horrendously honest. Whatever her dad and pa thought, she would never be as beautiful as they said she was.

After all, they stared at her through rose-tinted glasses. She was their whole world. She had completed their family. She was a gift, one they had never expected they would be allowed to receive. Or at least, that was what they told her. Of course they were going to be biased. She was their *daughter*.

Karen, at least, knew that she could have a more realistic opinion of herself. She couldn't trust her loving and doting parents to do that. They were blind to her faults. Heck, they would practically let her get away with murder if she managed to talk them around in the right way.

She shook her head and pushed the hair out of her face yet again. Taking a deep breath and resigned to her fate, Karen plodded onwards. It was time for her to head home, even if there were more hours in the day that she could use to work towards her goal. But, she mused, there were other things that she could at least try to do at home. There was still time before she would need to collapse into bed.

Her legs were no better; they were screaming out in agony. Her heart was trying to explode from her chest. She still felt like she was making little to no progress, even if she had run many a mile in just a single day.

Soon, though, she wouldn't have so much time to do this. It would be time to go back to school, to resume her studies along with her schoolmates. But, where many of her friends had firm ideas about where they wanted to go and what they wanted to do next, Karen was at a loss.

All she wanted was to be beautiful, in the hopes that then she would have a better understanding of who she was and what she wanted. Until then, she was just a mess of conflicting emotions in a world that made no sense.

Karen was certain that feeling right about herself on the outside would make sure that she knew what she wanted on the inside. It was logical, it made sense. Anybody who tried to claim otherwise was a fool.

The town streets were quiet as Karen wound her way through them towards the cul-de-sac she called home. She had lived here for as long as she could remember. It was the place where her dad had been born and she was certain that he would die here too.

A part of her found that sweet. The rest of her wanted to escape. She couldn't understand how being trapped in one place didn't drive her dad and pa insane. But Karen was young; of course they should have understood that she needed to roam the world.

After all, wasn't that what all kids wanted?

That was why she ran. It helped her to escape from the world, to find a way to get out of this cloying trap, and to make herself beautiful and slim to boot. Unfortunately, these days, she felt like a hamster on a wheel, spinning round and round but never getting anywhere.

Karen stopped when she reached her driveway to catch her breath. Their home was right at the end of the street and backed out onto a park. It was nice, quiet, but that wasn't always a good thing.

The lounge light was on and she could see the shadowy figures of her parents sitting behind them. She wondered what they were talking about, if it was just their days at work or if it was about her. But she wasn't a kid, they couldn't really be that worried, could they?

Lola, their black-and-white cat, was stretched out across the windowsill. Like always, she looked like she owned the place. Karen smiled. Out of her whole family, she was sure that Lola understood her best.

With a sigh of resignation, Karen knocked on the door. It may have been her own home, but she still hadn't been graced with the luxury of her own key yet. She was sure that her parents were determined to infantilise her for as long as feasibly possible.

"Karen, darling," Pa gushed as he threw the door open. Dad enveloped her into a tight hug at the same time. "Where have you been? We were so worried about you, weren't we, David?"

"Peter," Dad said cautiously as he held her at arm's length. "Give Karen some space. She's only just got back home."

Karen rolled her eyes. It was just like her dad to make a statement like that. He was the one touching her, invading her personal space. At least Pa was only cooing over her with affectionate words and worried eyes lined with crow's feet.

"I'm fine." Karen went to head upstairs, straight to her room, straight to that damned mirror, when both of them caught hold of her again.

"Karen...."

"I lost track of time, that's all." She let out a heavy breath through her nose. It whistled as she sighed. It was too big for her face, Karen thought bitterly. "Look, Dad, Pa, I'm really tired. Can't I just go to bed now?"

"But we haven't seen you all day."

Karen rolled her eyes, grabbed hold of the bannister and made her way upstairs. She didn't care what Dad and Pa had to say. Not right now, anyway. Her mind was elsewhere. And besides, every single muscle ached, her head was spinning, and she felt like she was going to be sick.

Who was she, anyway? What did she want from life? And why, when things were meant to be so easy, was everything so hard?

"I'm worried about her."

It was a simple statement. Peter nodded in agreement with his partner, handed over a cup of steaming hot tea and settled down on the leather sofa beside David. Lola was in the kitchen, crunching noisily on dry cat food, but to David, the house was still too eerily quiet.

"What happened to our little girl?"

"She's growing up, David." Peter's words hung in the air. Both of them knew there was far more to this situation than that. But neither of them wanted to actually say it because then and only then would it make it actually real.

David sighed heavily. "Dear, you know it isn't just that. She used to have dreams. Remember how she wanted to be a doctor when she was small? How she'd drag all of her teddies out and use all of the plasters on them as if to make them better." David sighed wistfully. "And then, when you'd cut yourself while chopping the veggies, you found out she'd used them all up?"

Peter's lips curled into a smile. "There was the time she wanted to be an astronaut, and ran around the house wearing that old fishbowl on her head."

"Don't forget her Pablo Picasso phase, the one where she absolutely wrecked her bedroom walls, scrawling all over them with marker pens." David let out a small laugh. "I swear we can still see it underneath the layers of paint we daubed over it."

They fell into an awkward silence, reminiscing. The truth was, it was far easier to think about better days than the issues they had now. David could feel his little Karen drifting further and further away from him and that only made things worse.

After all, how could he save her from the demons of the world if she wouldn't actually talk to him—talk to *either* of them—about it?

"She's too thin now."

Peter breathed heavily through his nose. It whistled. Lola jumped up onto the sofa, the cat looking desperately for a lap to sleep on. "I know," he whispered.

"She looks ill."

"I know."

"What do we do? How can we stop this?" David stood up, startling the cat, who bolted straight back up onto the windowsill.

"That, I don't know. I wish I did." Peter patted the sofa beside him, hoping that would encourage the man he loved to take a seat again. "We're her parents. We're meant to have all the solutions to her problems."

David ran a hand through his thinning hair. "She's nearly an adult herself now. Karen knows we're not completely infallible. She knows our family is, you know, different. And even then, I don't think that's the issue...."

"You wish you could get in her mind, figure it out and make it all better, don't you?"

"And you don't?"

"Of course I do, but forcing it makes it worse. It needs to come from an honest place, otherwise she'll only end up in a worse position than before."

"The counsellor in you is speaking again." David crossed his arms, but quickly relaxed them.

Peter grinned. "I know. It comes with the territory. Come on, sit down. I'll try and talk to her in the morning, before she goes out to do...whatever it is she's been doing all day lately."

David sighed. It wasn't much, but it was enough. He had to trust Peter to smooth this situation down. But talking to his daughter these days, it was like walking on eggshells.

He would do anything to have the old Karen back. The vibrant, happy girl who wanted to be a teacher one week and then a policewoman the next. Instead, she had been replaced with a little lost lamb with a despicable attitude. The door slamming and cold shoulders she gave them both were bad enough, but it was the hollow, blank look in Karen's eyes that haunted David more than anything else.

Some people insisted it was simply teenage years, puberty and hormones. But at least Peter agreed that there could, *could* be something a little more going on with their daughter.

The sooner they could solve this whole mess, the better.

When Karen woke at five a.m., everything ached. Her arms felt like they barely belonged to her; heavy and stiff, like they were made of solid granite. She sucked in a deep breath, blinking as the early morning sunlight invaded her senses.

Her head throbbed too; she swore that her eyes would burst out of their sockets at any given second. And her stomach gurgled emptily, threatening to spew bile up her oesophagus and out of her mouth.

Gritting her teeth, Karen slowly moved her arm and ran her fingers over her hollowed abdomen. It didn't feel right. Sometimes, she swore it would never feel right.

After all, nothing about her was right, from the inside to the out.

Was it worth her even getting up in the mornings? What was the point in her being alive, even?

Her birth mother had the right idea. She had gotten rid of her as soon as feasibly possible. Made her dad and her pa be the ones who were responsible for bringing up the atrocity that was Karen Wilkinson.

She felt sorry for them. They were good people; they hadn't ever deserved to be encumbered with a burden such as herself. If she weren't in the equation, then their lives would have been far easier. It was only natural, after all.

Because, really, there wasn't anywhere in the world she belonged.

This time of day, when the sun was just beginning to peek over the hills outside, was when she felt most comfortable. At this time of day, it was easier to disappear, to feel like she was barely there. Like she was maybe just a figment of somebody's imagination, or a ghost, waiting to creak the floorboards or squeak through the open doors.

Why did living have to be so difficult, anyway?

Although everything still hurt, Karen blindly groped at her side table. She needed to do something about this. The pain was getting too much. She was sick of disappointing everyone she cared about. Fed up with being a waste of space. Tired of getting in the way all of the time.

Plus, there was the mirror. The mirror and its taunts. She was grotesque. She was barely human. She looked like an alien. She was disgusting. She was a disappointment in the whole scheme of human evolution.

What was the point in even trying if she was never going to win, anyway?

Finally, her fingers skittered over the slim, stainless steel object she was looking for. The nail scissors were so innocuous. They had a singular use and nobody ever believed they could really do any serious damage to anyone.

After all, they were only designed with cutting nails in mind.

But Karen knew. She had done this before. On times like this when she felt—no, she *knew*—that the light at the end of the tunnel was slowly disappearing. That all hope was leaving her to wallow in the depths of an unending blackness.

The first cut, she knew from prior experience, was always the hardest.

But, but, but....

It was one of the few things she was able to do these days. Besides, what harm would it do to anyone but herself?

The Curious Antiquities Shop

Dust motes hung in the air as Lucy took a tentative step over the threshold and into the shop. She shivered. A part of her felt like the place was calling her, saying *come hither, come on, you can do it, you want to see, you* need *to see.*

The rest wanted to promptly turn on her heels and run for dear life.

She wasn't sure what to make of this place. It had been there for as long as she could remember. Lucy had passed it so many times, without giving it even a second glance. It was part of the furniture, something that nobody thought twice about. Like a dusty old chest of drawers, casually stuffed into a corner and never disturbed.

Or the old bookshelf, filled to the brim with classics that nobody bothered to touch.

Passers-by always seemed to complain about the place. They said it was an eyesore and needed demolishing. The shop was a waste of space, a unit that could be put to good use as something else.

As what? Lucy thought. Another charity shop? A hairdresser's, a beautician's? Yet another café, or—heaven forbid—a Costa, a Starbucks? Or worse, a pound shop?

She shuddered at the thought. Town centres were becoming interchangeable with one another; a cardboard cut-out that could be replicated again and again. Places like this, at least, offered a break from the monotony and gave towns a different character.

After all, where else could she find such a unique assortment of bits and pieces?

Even after having glanced in the window from time to time, as days turned into weeks, weeks into months, and those months into old seasons, Lucy knew that the stock changed. She doubted that you would see the same thing twice, if you came in here on a regular basis.

She shook her head. Why had it taken her so long to come inside?

Edgar, Edgar and Sons was like a throwback to another time, another era. Lucy, with her mobile phone in one hand and a Bag for Life in the other, always felt like she would break the illusion of time travel if she entered. As a consequence, she shied away and studiously avoided the place. She had wanted to imagine that the dark, twisting corridors would be something out of the Victorian era, with curious oddities just waiting patiently to be discovered.

Lucy ran her index finger across an ornate chest of drawers with floral engravings in the ebony wood. She blew the dust off of her fingertip and looked at the line which shined bright against the rest of the piece of furniture. She felt rebellious, like she was destroying the passage of time that had occurred within *Edgar, Edgar and Sons*.

"Can I help you?"

Lucy wheeled around at the sound of the voice. It was creaky, old, like the items that were up for sale. But it was equally warm, friendly, and inviting.

She blinked and wondered why it had taken her so long to come inside.

"Dear?" the voice prompted after she failed to reply.

"I...I'm fine," Lucy stammered. She shook her head, her tightly curled black hair bouncing on her shoulders. "Just browsing, thank you."

For a moment, Lucy absorbed the appearance of the person standing in front of her. The woman, she looked like she had stepped out of the same era as the rest of the place. Lucy felt underdressed, like she should go home, find an ornate corset and shawl, and wear a magnificent wig. Maybe even carry around one of those masks on sticks which people used to wear at masquerade balls.

The woman nodded. "Well, okay, dear. Let me know if you change your mind."

Lucy nodded as the woman readjusted her crocheted black shawl over her shoulders and disappeared into the shadowy depths of the shop. One moment her feet had been shuffling along the dirty parquet flooring, and the next, she was gone.

Stepping forward nervously, Lucy traced the woman's steps. It was like she had literally disappeared into the aether. Like she had jumped into another universe or disapparated *à la* Harry Potter.

Lucy wheeled around the corner. She swore she would find this woman if she just got around there faster. Almost tripping over her feet in haste, Lucy frowned when she came to a dead end.

Especially so as it was a dead end with no elderly woman straightening out her shawl.

However, Lucy let out a laugh when she saw, on a long thin stick, a masquerade mask, just like the one she had been imagining only minutes earlier.

With quivering fingers, Lucy reached out for it. She had to roll up onto her tiptoes; it was positioned precariously high, buried amongst various old hats and furs. Still, as her fingers tightened in grip around the stick, she grinned.

Grinned, and then promptly coughed. A flurry of dust kicked up as Lucy knocked the hats rolling back down onto the floor. It was snowing dust now. She laughed again, almost uncontrollably. This seemed like the kind of thing that could only happen in fairy tales.

Because, really, disappearing old women and the items you were imagining suddenly appearing out of nowhere were the stuff of Disney films.

Taking deep breaths, she managed to calm herself and really look at the object in her hands. She twirled it around in the half-light. They were partially cast in shadows; the sunlight only just filtered through into the far depths of the shop. Lucy could have been buried far inside any old abandoned building. The weird and wonderful collection of objects didn't help much, either.

She strained her head, trying to hear. Lucy needed some sort of confirmation that she wasn't quite as utterly alone as she felt right now. She clutched hold of the mask for dear life, as if it was anchoring her to the world.

There was no noise apart from the rhythmic thrumming of her heart, though. The absence of any other sound was what was most startling. No susurration of people muttering mindless remarks to one another, no roar of traffic from the road outside, and not even any birds calling hauntingly to one another in the distance.

Letting out a heavy sigh, Lucy made a mental note to pull herself together. She was overreacting. The only reason why *Edgar, Edgar and Sons* was so quiet was because it wasn't exactly popular. It was just there, part of the furniture, as it were. Half the reason she had come in at all was because she wanted an escape and reprieve from the day-to-day worries that pestered the passers-by on the street.

The mask in her hand was beautiful. Royal blue with ornate peacock feathers that once stood proudly. Now, they hung a little limp, but it looked like they were trying desperately to maintain the regality they held in yesteryear. Silvery and emerald gemstones, likely only costume jewellery gems, decorated the mask, adding a little bit of glitter to the proceedings. A few had become loose, two were missing entirely, but somehow the flaws only added to its charms.

It was simultaneously ostentatious and gaudy, whilst being beautiful and ornate. Lucy wasn't entirely sure what to make of it. However, she didn't feel like she could leave the shop without having it with her.

It didn't matter that she had no need for it. It didn't matter that she wouldn't have any use for it, not even for a costume party. Even the price had faded back into irrelevancy. Lucy knew she had to take this thing with her, otherwise she would regret it for the rest of her life.

She didn't understand where the sudden conviction to purchase it had come from. Maybe there was something in the air; a little magic alongside all the dust motes. It wasn't normally her thing, especially not when there were books she had been planning to buy. Lucy didn't have that much disposable income. In fact, she had been planning to spend the money left over from bills on her mum's birthday present this month.

Still, she vowed she would make ends meet. The mask was coming with her.

She turned on her heels and strode out of the dead end. Swiftly, determinedly, Lucy retraced her steps until she was more or less at the spot where she had first met the old lady.

Everything seemed slightly different, but she went on unperturbed.

After all, the woman had sought her out in this deathly quiet shop. Presumably, she was the owner of *Edgar, Edgar and Sons*, but she couldn't discount her being a very elderly sales assistant. Whatever the woman's role, Lucy knew she needed to talk to her. But where to look? The woman couldn't have disappeared into thin air, could she?

Lucy cleared her throat, blinked, and let out a breath. She held onto her new prize as if it could disappear from within her grasp in seconds.

After all, *Edgar, Edgar and Sons* was a rather strange shop and she was beginning to think that anything could happen here. It almost wouldn't surprise her if the walls started moving and the old woman who ran the shop changed into a dashing young man.

She looked pointedly at the stacks of antiques and curios beside her. None were familiar, but as she had wandered through this place, she hadn't really been paying any attention. Really, Lucy had just wandered aimlessly. She hadn't even realised she was looking for a masquerade ball mask until she clapped eyes on it.

Had everything in this shop really completely changed? Lucy couldn't remember having seen them before, but that didn't exactly mean much. *Edgar, Edgar and Sons* was rather dark and she was only starting to focus properly on her surroundings now.

Still, the fact of the matter was that there was only one consistency. Everywhere Lucy looked, there were dust motes that hung in the air like glitter, illuminated by the scant slivers of light that made it through the furniture.

"Ma'am?" she questioned, feeling a little foolish. It was like she was speaking into air and hoping that a ghost would appear before her. Or like she had been handed one of those trick boxes, which required a little thought to solve them. Her mum was great at solving those things, she would love one.

But for now, Lucy just wanted to get out of this shop and return to normality. She wanted to stuff her new treasure in the pound shop bag and make her way home. There, she could recount her experience within this antiques and curios shop on Facebook. Maybe she would encourage her friends to come and have a look, to solve the puzzle and, if not, just have a laugh.

However, *Edgar, Edgar and Sons* was surprisingly large. It was like a maze and every turn she took, Lucy felt like she was getting further and further from the exit.

And even if she did find the exit, she needed to see the old lady first. She didn't want to leave the mask behind. She just wanted to pay and get out of here for now.

There had been more than enough curiosity for one day. *Curiosity killed the cat*, she remembered. The words whispered through her mind and sent a shiver down her spine.

Another turn and the door stood in front of her, proud and firm. Light shone on the entrance mat; it was a honey trap, one which a cat would have loved to curl up in.

On the bookshelf to the left of the door was a trick box. Lucy couldn't even begin to guess exactly how old it was. Made out of a dark wood, it was ornately decorated, carved with fine pictures of satyrs, elves, and centaurs. Fictional characters; the perfect representation of the unknown, of fairy tales, whimsy, and curiosity.

But there was no old woman.

Lucy looked at the mask in her hand, with its dulled sequins and drooping peacock feathers. She glanced at the trick box. Her mum would love that. She knew it. She remembered story times from long ago, when her mother invented magical creatures and crazy tales to lull her daughter to sleep.

She missed those days.

With a sigh, Lucy reached out with the hand still holding the mask. It quivered above the shelf as she tried to make a decision. She was at a crossroads; to continue to search out for the shop owner, whoever that may be, or to put everything down and run.

Run back to normalcy.

Put *Edgar, Edgar and Sons*, and the supposed waste of commercial space that it was, behind her.

Did she really need the masquerade mask? Did she want it so badly now? Or had the sunlight made her come to her senses?

Lucy dropped it beside the trick box. The place was getting under her skin. There was no sign of the owner, or anybody else for that matter. She was alone in this ghost of a shop and needed to get out of here. It wasn't worth searching, not anymore.

She opened the door and fled.

Later, when Lucy got home and almost all thoughts of *Edgar, Edgar and Sons* had been eradicated from her mind, she froze. On her desk was the mask, sitting neatly beside the curious trick box that she had specifically left behind.

Second Glance

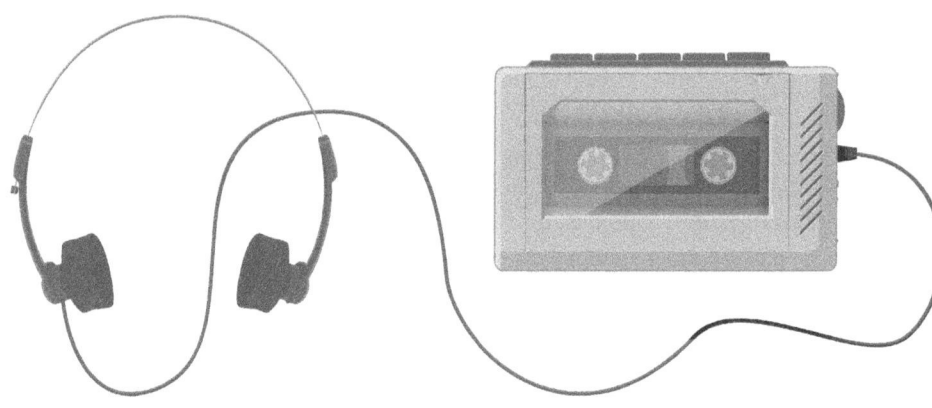

Elena walked down the street, head ducked low, with hands buried deep within her pockets. Headphones, the old metal style with padding over the tiny speakers, were clamped tightly over her navy bobble hat. She looked so patently outdated and so out of fashion that she seemed like she came from another era. She made it look effortlessly cool again.

Likewise, she used a cassette player and was proud of the fact. It had been practically given to her at a yard sale. The original owner was surprised to even get a few pennies from it. In truth, they had been expecting to throw it away at the end of the day, alongside the empty milk bottles and tin cans.

For Elena, though, the silver-and-blue plastic contraption had been love at first sight. One second, she had been cassette player-less and the next, she couldn't imagine her life without it. She needed the thing, more than she had needed anything before. Even if the old owner, a scruffy man more than three times her own age, had blatantly overpriced it, Elena would have still happily bought it.

To her, it was priceless.

Bradley knew that.

Bradley knew because he was there when it had happened. He'd seen the transaction occur from upstairs in his bedroom window. The scruffy man was his father and Bradley had been under strict instructions to keep out of the way at all costs. His father didn't want him under his feet.

But Bradley hadn't been able to take his eyes off the pretty girl with luminescent skin, hazel eyes and long, straight, black hair. He'd watched as her hands quivered with excitement as she dropped the pennies into Bradley's father's hands.

He'd watched as she practically bounced away up the street, clutching her new purchase for dear life.

For six months, he'd been trying to track her down again. He hadn't been able to get the beautiful girl walking away with his old cassette player out of his mind. She haunted his dreams and his waking thoughts too. So many people scoffed at the idea of love at first sight, but not Bradley.

He was infatuated with the image of this perfect girl who had turned up at his dad's yearly house clear out.

Only last week had he come across her again, at school. It took him by surprise. How could he have attended the same school as her for so long, without them having even crossed paths once within the past six months?

Had he not been paying attention? Was Elena hiding from him? Or was he just invisible to her, and thus, the same occurred vice versa. Perhaps they passed each other by, like two ships in the night, only narrowly avoiding making contact.

How desperate he was for them to collide. It would be a thing of beauty. He knew it would be. He didn't have to *know* her to understand what she was like.

But now, he had seen her and he knew that he hadn't been imagining some kind of fantasy girl. It was the look in her eye, the slight frown and the way she chewed the insides of her cheeks as she focused. Bradley wondered if she made herself bleed by doing that.

He wondered what kind of music she listened to on the cassette player, too.

During the week, he had made her countless mixtapes, featuring all his favourite songs. He only had a radio and cassette player himself; it wasn't too much of a hardship to do. Bradley hoped she'd like them. His taste was eclectic, to say the least; jazz, R 'n' B, rock, country and western, a little classical, and more. She had to like at least some of the tracks. Really, he hoped she'd like them all.

He imagined she'd be a cat person. The aloof and superior nature of them would probably suit her down to the ground. Her favourite ice cream was most likely butterscotch; sweet, but with a little salty touch that lifted it above the ordinary. Something unusual, not the typical vanilla that everybody ate but nobody particularly loved.

Elena clearly spent most of her time alone. It wasn't because nobody liked her, but because they didn't understand her. But he would; he could get her just as she would know him. All he had to do was catch her attention.

And yet, she never seemed to look twice at him. Bradley might as well have been invisible.

Was it his ratty black hair, the mole on his left cheek, or the fact his clothes were worn? Those things, though, were usually what made him stand out. It was why the kids at school taunted and teased him. They ridiculed him even when he tried to make an effort. And he did try desperately to make things better. But, however hard he tried, his father always undid all of his hard work.

All Bradley wanted to do, though, was to escape.

And if he got to escape with someone as beautiful and alluring as Elena, then, all the better it would be for him.

But they were just kids. His mum wasn't on the scene. He'd tried to track her down, to no avail. Used social media, hoping to get people to share his plea and his plight around the world. He'd scoured the papers, made calls to his paternal grandparents, and more. None of it worked.

Instead, he made his situation worse and he had the scars to prove it.

Even so, there was nothing wrong with living with hope. It wouldn't be too long until he was old enough to walk away and never return. Then his father would never see him again, and even then, *never* would still be far too soon.

He sighed heavily and plodded his way down the street. Elena took up too much of his mind. Bradley knew he shouldn't be daydreaming about her like this, not when he had more important things to worry about.

Like getting back home again, weighed down by a menagerie of groceries that he doubted they even needed at home. But his father insisted. And if Bradley's father insisted, then really, it was a demand, not a request. Again, he had the scars to prove it.

His trainers were falling apart. Bradley didn't dare ask for a new pair, because then he would be allegedly proving that he was ungrateful and surly and rude and an insult to the family name. He was apparently lucky that he even had a pair of trainers at all. But the soles were peeling off and the laces were barely long enough to tie up these days.

But staring at his feet was better than the alternative. Staring at his feet meant that no well-meaning stranger would question the bruise blossoming on his forehead.

The sole flipped under his feet, in spite of him keeping a careful watch over them. Bradley tripped forward several steps. The ground was getting closer and closer to his face and his arms cartwheeled as he tried to regain his balance.

And then, he stopped falling. The ground didn't get any closer to his face but it didn't get any further away, either.

Somebody had caught him. Somebody had stopped the embarrassment. Someone had prevented the otherwise inevitable injury, one which could have delayed his getting home in good time, at least according to his father.

He looked up in a blurry haze and couldn't focus on the eyes looking back down at him. Bradley blinked, let his eyes refocus and took a second glance. Slack-jawed and gobsmacked, he couldn't believe who it was who'd caught him.

Elena. In her long black hair and hazel-eyed perfection. With tanned, glowing skin and the old metal headphones that his dad used to have glued to his head practically 24 hours a day, 7 days a week.

Elena, with her crooked smile and slightly off-centre nose. Elena and her willowy long legs and arms, all disguised underneath thick swathes of clothes.

The girl he had been dreaming of for all this time.

Bradley could scarcely believe it. If he hadn't humiliated himself in front of her, he might have been thrilled by the serendipity of finally having an excuse to talk to her. If he hadn't just been saved from cracking his nose on the pavement and adding to his extensive list of scars and injuries, then he would have delighted in the opportunity to finally talk to Elena.

She smiled at him. Crookedly, of course. Bradley felt like his heart skipped several beats at once. It was worth it, always. "Hey, you okay?" she asked, raising a perfect eyebrow. Elena's hand moved to the cassette player and she switched it off.

How could he respond? Bradley was standing there, gaping, like a goldfish. Times like this, he wanted the world to swallow him whole. The colour rose to his cheeks, red hot and full of fire. Whenever he blushed, he turned into a tomato.

"Hey," Elena repeated. "Breathe, you're okay, okay? You're the Watkins kid, aren't you? Brian?"

"Bradley," he corrected, finally managing to find where he had buried his voice. "I'm Bradley."

"Cool. I'm Elena. I've seen you around. You want to go for a coffee or something? Looks like you could do with a rest. You're pretty loaded."

The groceries were scattered around their feet. Immediately, Bradley fell to his knees and started to gather it up. He hoped, prayed even, that nothing was damaged. If it was, then there would be damage done to something else.

Elena bent down to help. It was only seconds until their hands brushed against one another. Bradley froze, blushed, and looked away.

"Hey, that's all your stuff, okay?" Elena said hastily, handing him the last apple. "Um, hey, you didn't answer. Would you like that coffee? It's okay to say no, okay?"

"I...." His tongue felt thick with cotton. "I'd like to. Really, I would."

"Cool. Here, give me one of your bags, okay?"

Bradley smiled. He had so many questions for her. He needed to get to know the *real* her. The fictional Elena in his head needed to be replaced with the one of flesh and blood standing in front of him. It had taken so long for him to finally find her, to actually be able to talk to her. It had taken so long for her to take that second glance at him.

He knew it was worth it.

He couldn't even think about anything else right now. All thoughts of his father escaped his mind. Sooner, rather than later, he would escape his father's grasp. For now, he had more important things to worry about.

It was about time he grabbed hold of his own life before it was taken from him.

"Hey, um, Elena?"

"Yes?" She quirked an eyebrow at him again. His legs turned to jelly. For a second, Bradley thought he was going to fall all over again.

"So, are you a cat person or a dog person?" Bradley blurted the words out before he even had a chance to really think about it. It didn't matter, not in the greater scheme of things. He didn't even know why it was the first thing he needed to ask her.

Elena chuckled and brushed a strand of hair behind her ear. Her hazel eyes sparkled. The metal band of the headphones pressed against her neck. She was a picture of perfection.

"Neither. I'm a rabbit person."

Bradley balked for a second. Yes, he definitely had a lot to learn about the real Elena. But it didn't matter. He could already tell that nothing about her would be a disappointment.

How could it be? She was perfectly imperfect. And she danced to the beat of her own drum. And she didn't look at him like he was scum of the earth.

He barely knew her, but as their fingers found one another, Bradley swore that he had known Elena all his life.

Beyond the Veil

They say that hearing is the last thing to go before you die.

I mean, everyone says it, like it's some kind of God-given fact. What proof is out there for it? I mean, seriously. Surely it should be something like touch that goes last. Of course, you're always touching something, even if you are lying in a hospital bed and all you can feel is the rough gown and cotton sheets they have you wrapped up in. Even if all you are vaguely aware of is the feel of tubes pumping chemicals and stuff into your body, or keeping your lungs going, or heart pounding, or whatever.

Seriously, surely the last thing to go should be the sense of touch.

At least, that is what I always used to think.

I'd scoff and roll my eyes whenever people said hearing is the last thing to go. Because, for somebody who's deaf, it definitely isn't, for a start. And, I mean, you hear about people losing their senses of taste, smell, and eyesight too. But never the sense of touch. Even people who are born deaf-blind, you hear about people raising money for sensory rooms so they can be kind of, you know, involved in the world through touch.

So yeah, I always thought that touch would be the last to go.

Until...

Until...

Until it was *my* turn to die.

Don't get me wrong. I mean, I wasn't ever afraid of death. I *mean*, what a waste of time is that, eh? It's like, I don't know, being afraid of sleeping or breathing or whatever. Being afraid of dying makes more sense because, y'know, it involves pain. Probably. Usually. Whatever.

Anyway, death is one of those inevitable things in life. You're born and you will die. It's whatever is in between that's the scary stuff. What you make of life, crap like that. Whether or not you fall in love, become a criminal, win the Nobel Peace Prize, or are brutally and horrifically murdered by a crazed stalker. It could happen. It could all happen. When you're born, the sky is the limit. Proverbially speaking. And even then, aeroplanes are a thing. Rocket ships are too.

So yeah, that's what I mean. In life, anything can happen. And that, that is terrifying. There's so much any one person can do and you're like, you know, guaranteed not to be able to fit it all in. That's one thing that definitely, definitely is impossible.

Death, meanwhile, *will* happen. Sooner or later, it happens to all of us. We're not immortal; we can't keep going and going and going forever.

Besides, how boring would that be? Living forever, I mean. Even the most exciting things in the world would become samey and old and mundane and, yeah, well, boring.

And who would want to live forever anyway? 'Cause you'd watch all the people you know and love grow old and die, while you keep going on and on and on. Loss would be like a constant companion, if you know what I mean. I'd hate that. Seeing everyone I love die and having no escape route myself.

Can't say I wouldn't have minded a little more time, though. For living, I mean. Because yeah, there's always that little bit more you could wish you did.

And yeah, for someone like me, it's kind of a wish that there was a lot more I could do.

But I guess there's no point in wishing for something like that. It's as pointless as wishing on a star. When, all a star is, is just a big hunk of gas burning, doing nuclear fusion, because all it is, is a stupid ongoing chemical reaction that happens, simply because. It's not going to grant wishes because it isn't sentient. It's only chemicals, chemistry.

And anyway, all of that is so beside the point.

The point is, yeah, hearing. It being the last sense we lose before we die. Okay, okay, so I'm no scientist, I never had the chance, you see, but how can anyone prove that? Reanimation isn't real and even if it was, yeah, look, zombies. Frankenstein's monster. That kind of thing. Sometimes, fiction has more answers for the unknown than reality.

Look, here, now, I can speak from experience. All those people. All those claims and all that, yeah. They were right. It seems mad, but it's true.

Hearing is the last sense to go. Well, obviously not if you are deaf because, well, that's kinda obvious, isn't it? But yeah, for me, a normal hearing person who happens to have died, passed on, kicked the bucket, and all of those other clichés for death, hearing was the last thing I lost.

And you know what?

More than anything, I wish I'd lost it sooner. Because honestly, it would have made things so much better for me in those last few moments in the land of the living.

I mean, don't get me wrong. Losing your hearing sucks. Losing your sight sucks too. Those times when people say would you prefer to be blind or deaf, I'd always say neither. Yeah, people can roll their eyes at me all they want, but who would *want* to be either?

But in this case, just before death, it would have been so much easier for me.

I guess you need a little of my history so you know why. Why I would have been so much happier to lose my hearing well before I died.

Story's simple enough, I guess.

Cancer. Hodgkin's lymphoma. A cruel, evil disease that cuts down people before they even have a chance to grow.

I mean, you didn't really think I was an elderly lady, did you? You couldn't have possibly believed that I'd had a chance to really experience the world, to really live, did you? Course not, that would have been dumb.

I mean, yeah, I know I'm still just a kid. Or was, whatever. Does it make any difference now that I'm dead, anyway? I know that means you probably think that I believe I know it all and that adults, my 'elders' haven't a clue about the way things work. Yeah, you probably think I'm some snotty little brat now who is using her sob story only to get your attention.

And, yeah, so what if I am? The point is, I have to talk to somebody about it. I mean, yeah, you wouldn't have been my first choice. There're plenty of people I would much rather have spoken to about this. And I know you definitely don't want to be hearing about the whines and whinges of a kid who is already dead, do you? Not exactly the best dinnertime conversational material, is it?

Anyway. Yeah. Cancer is a bitch and the treatments for it are worse. It strips you of everything that makes you human, all just to try and cling on to a few more years. Years of what? Pain, exhaustion, and all of that? Or actual proper life because the cancer cells were all killed and enough of whatever makes you *you* manages to cling on through the brutal treatments?

Clearly, it was a waste of time and money and energy in my case. I'm already dead, aren't I? Would've been better just to let the cancer win instead of trying to kill all the bad cells and leave all the good ones behind. Chemotherapy is indiscriminate; it picks off both just because it can.

And as for radiation? Well, let's just use something that can cause cancer to kill it? Some kind of fight-fire-with-fire nonsense right there.

Still, I went through it all and the disease won out. Broke my parents' hearts and my younger sister's too. At least I think it did. I hope it did. Damn it, I mean, I need to be remembered by somebody, don't I?

I mean, they're all I had left in the world. Cancer didn't just strip me of me, but of my whole friendship circle and everything. I was alienated from them, I was different, they couldn't relate. So friends, everyone except my closest family drifted away, one by one.

They were replaced by cold, steely doctors. People who were doing their worst to me to try to save me. They didn't care about me the person, they just wanted to make sure I survived so they'd be the hero in my little story.

Heh, so much for that and for them.

Still, I could hear what they were saying.

All of them.

I might not have been able to smell them or see them or, you know. But, yeah, I mean, what I'm trying to say is, I knew they were there because I could hear them.

That's all I had left. In those last few hours, those last few minutes, all I could hear was what they were saying. I could hear the creak of doors being opened and shut. The regular bleeping of machines measuring my vitals. And yeah, what the nurses and the doctors were saying around me.

My family didn't make it to my bedside in time. You know what I mean, yeah? None of them made it.

But I wasn't alone. I was with nurses. People who were supposed to care as they monitored the life as it drained out of my very body. People who were meant to have a passion for the job, a vocation, whatever.

And I needed them, damn it. More than that, really. I needed their support, their compassion as I left this world for, well, whatever. You'll find out soon enough, I guess.

You want to know what the very last words I heard were? Really? Fine, if you must.

But bear in mind, I knew what I looked like in a mirror. In that great wide beyond, what I'd once been, I still knew. Cancer may have stolen everything else from me, but I damn well still had my memories. Have, whatever. Cause, you know, I can recall all this and I have told you it and yeah.

Anyway. Those last words.

"God, isn't she ugly?"

Imagine that being the last thing you heard. Imagine knowing they are talking about you. Imagine knowing that they are probably right because even your reflection looks alien to you because of all the supposed treatments. Just imagine.

Imagine having that tormenting you through the pain of dying.

Imagine that always lingering in your mind in the afterlife. Or whatever it is, anyway.

I mean, you don't expect me to tell you what to expect after it all ends, do you? Not after what you said to me as I was dying, damn it.

Words, they can cut through people like knives. Words can kill. You better be careful what you say. You never know what might haunt you for all of days.

So, you just imagine that.

Seeing the Light

"Mr. Wilkinson." The young woman proffered a well-manicured hand with dainty fingernails. Tentatively, Peter shook it. "It's good to see you again."

He nodded in response. This chit of a girl, she looked barely older than his Karen. How could she be a working woman, how could he trust her to help? How could she even be out of school?

And yet, there she was, standing before him with a benign smile. Sophie Anders probably couldn't believe that he had dared come back. The corners of her eyes were slightly crooked. Her face was relaxed but her hands were balled up tightly. Yes, she was relieved he was back again. She wanted to help.

But how could she?

How could she piece together their lives again? How could this young girl even start to put his mind back together? How could she help his relationship with his daughter and husband? Ever since Karen had been hospitalised, it seemed like everything had gone from bad to worse.

It was a wonder that David could even tolerate him these days.

It was his fault Karen had become so ill. He was the counsellor; he could have–*should* have–been able to see all the signs. Her behaviour, in retrospect, it was all so obvious. But that was the problem with hindsight, wasn't it? Always twenty-twenty vision; that was what people said about it.

And Sophie, this poor young girl, she had to offer counselling to a counsellor. It was like a doctor administrating medical care to another doctor. Peter knew that he was most probably the worst kind of customer this kid could have.

As he climbed upstairs, knowing she was only a step behind him, Peter sighed. He had to stop thinking of Sophie –*his* counsellor–as being a child. He needed to remind himself that she was not one of Karen's peers and not a representation of his failure as a father.

But every single time he looked into those earnest eyes, so desperate to help piece him back together again, his mind drifted back to his daughter. How could everything have ended up this way?

When, exactly, did the tables turn? Why did he end up here? What was going on in his life?

Peter knew for certain, however, exactly who was responsible for this pickle.

That was him and him only.

If only he had taken note of Karen's illness. If only he had listened to David's concerns and pleas instead of brushing them under the carpet. If only he could stop blaming himself for everything that had happened.

It wasn't his fault, they said. But it was. That was what he kept telling himself. That anxious little itch in the back of his mind which grew louder as the world silenced. It didn't leave him alone; it couldn't, it *wouldn't* let him go.

As he sat down, he was wringing his hands again. Peter hadn't noticed he was doing it. At least, not until Sophie's eyes were drawn to his hands. He knew she didn't mean to stare, but she couldn't help it. It was kind of obvious, after all.

"So, Peter," Sophie started. Her voice was quiet, almost tentative. She was too new to this game. And he, he was a difficult customer. Peter knew he wouldn't want to be in her shoes.

After all, he hadn't been able to work in months. If he couldn't hold it together himself, how could he be paid to listen and help other people through the problems that life threw at them? He was a fraud and that, as they said, was that.

"Peter? How has this week been?" Sophie was quiet and softly spoken. Her words drifted over him like a wash of warm water. The room was quiet and peaceful.

It only served to highlight just how chaotic his head was, though.

"Hmm? Oh, much the same. How has your week been?"

He was lying. If only by omission, but a lie was still a lie. It was one of the characteristics he and David had ensured they had guided Karen away from since she had entered their lives. The pang of guilt gnawed away at the pit of his stomach. No wonder his husband found him to be unrecognisable these days.

Sophie smiled wanly. "I'm fine, thank you. How about your daughter and husband?"

Karen was better now. Or at least, according to society's standards, she was better. She no longer starved herself silly. She didn't force herself to vomit on a regular basis. And as for exercise? Of course Karen still worked out, but not to the foolish extremes that she once did.

But every single time Peter looked into his daughter's eyes, he could see the demons gnawing away behind them. He sincerely doubted that she would ever have a healthy relationship with food again. Eating was a challenge. The mirror was her mortal enemy.

And he, he had failed to notice. He hadn't given his daughter the right tools to live. David had noticed. David had urged Peter to step in, to help. Peter had held out, refused to believe there was anything wrong with their perfect little girl, one who was now training to be a dietician. One day, she said, she wanted to specialise in nutrition for athletes.

David, who was his rock and life, was drifting away with each and every day. The tighter that Peter tried to cling to him, the further away he seemed to be. Peter had nearly lost his daughter, but now he was on the verge of losing his husband.

"Hmm." Sophie tapped a pencil against her notepad. She still hadn't written anything down. "Did you manage to visit Karen at university this week? I believe you mentioned your intention to see her during our previous session."

"I, well, yes."

"And how did it go?"

"It was fine." Peter stammered as he spoke. The three words felt like they were stuck to the roof of his mouth. He was lying by omission again.

Of course, it had been wonderful to see his daughter. The house was so empty without her. Especially since the cat, Lola, had died. David had been heartbroken by that loss; he seemed sadder about that than the wreckage that was their marriage.

"Really?" Sophie sighed and folded her hands on the clipboard. The pencil was no longer a welcome distraction for this awkward conversation. "Peter, I cannot help you if you don't want to be helped."

"I know," he replied, miserable. He knew this game too well. Every cliché about counselling and depression there was in the book, he swore he was exhibiting each and every one of them now. "It's hard, you know?"

"I understand. But whatever has happened, whatever is happening and whatever *will* happen, you can cope with this. You've made the first step. You've come here."

Peter had heard himself say those words so many times in the past. He'd meant them too. He knew that young Sophie was being totally earnest when she said them. It might as well have come straight from a book called *Counselling for Dummies*.

But the words, he knew from experience, were meant to be a salve. They were meant to offer the recipient comfort and confidence. Peter knew that, in coming here and continuing his attendance with the counsellor, he was doing the right thing. But it didn't change anything. It didn't actually make him feel any better.

However, he was also sick and tired of feeling lousy and useless all of the time. He was a drain on society; a drain on David; a drain on every single person he had ever known. And he was so tired. All Peter wanted was for all of this to simply end.

He had been seeing Sophie for three months already. Each time he saw her, he was astounded by just how young she was, with her porcelain skin, perfect face, perfect hair and perfect nails. She looked like a model; like she belonged in a glass cage to stop anyone from hurting her.

Yet she was old enough to be a working woman. She was old enough to be a fully qualified counsellor. Peter knew from very personal experience that Sophie would have already heard all sorts of horror stories. And right now, she was listening–or not, as the case currently was–to the prattling of an old and decrepit man.

Still, in the not-too-distant future, once she had finished her training, his daughter could be astounding people in exactly the same way. And she looked healthy, she looked strong, she was a force to be reckoned with, in spite of all her demons.

"Peter?" Sophie prompted gently, "Please, talk to me. What's on your mind?"

"I let her down." He sucked in a deep breath. He wasn't going to break; he wasn't going to cry in front of this young girl, who was so keen to help him. "My husband, he knew there was something wrong and I ignored him. I let them down and now, now I'm just useless to them. I'm a waste of space."

"Hmm, is that what they've actually said to you? Or is that what you believe?"

"They don't need to say anything, just look at me."

Sophie did. Peter felt like her eyes were crawling over him. He saw her judging each and every pore. She was scrutinising him, just as he asked her to. He regretted it now. He wished he could find a hole to crawl into, to hide like a hermit. Maybe then the world would stop hurting him quite so much.

Isolation, even from those he loved, that was the very least he deserved at a time like this.

"I see a man who is blaming himself for things that were out of his control. I see a man who loves his husband and daughter more than anything else in the world. I see a man who thinks he let them down and is putting words in their mouths. I see a man who—"

"Sophie...." She was breaking all the rules. You never told the client how they were feeling. It was her inexperience, he figured, but didn't dare to say another word.

"I'm sorry," she muttered and cast her eyes down. But she didn't actually have anything to be sorry for. He'd asked for her opinion and she'd given it quite frankly. Yes, she should have known better, but he was almost grateful to hear her honest report.

"No, I'm sorry. I shouldn't be wasting your time."

"You came for a reason. You needed someone to talk to." Sophie's voice cracked a little as she spoke.

"Yes." She was right. There was no point in arguing with the facts.

"Have you actually spoken to your husband about... about what happened with your daughter? Have you talked now that she is in recovery?"

"Well, no. We don't really talk much at all."

"Does he blame you for Karen's illness?" Peter flinched. Even after these few weeks, he still wasn't used to hearing his daughter's name on Sophie's lips. The first few sessions, when they had covered Karen's eating disorder and recovery, had been torturous. He still hadn't really come to terms with it. All too often, he didn't think he ever would.

"I don't...."

"I'm sorry, but," Sophie paused, sucking in a deep breath, "I'm sorry, but if you don't talk to him, then you can't know exactly how he feels. You stood together while Karen was recovering and are still together now. David hasn't abandoned you and your daughter is okay. He's still supporting you, even now, as you blame yourself for something you couldn't have stopped."

Peter sat, stumped. Sophie was only stating the obvious, but sometimes the obvious was all that was needed. Sometimes your vision was too clouded to see exactly what was in front of you. He wasn't being stupid; depression was a very real thing. His GP wouldn't have suggested counselling in the first place if he didn't need that specific kind of treatment.

But he was pulling away from the people he loved. Out of what? Fear? Of rejection, of having his thoughts confirmed as being 'correct', of anger, frustration and retribution? Or just so that he could wallow in self-pity?

He needed to talk. Sophie was helping. He trusted her. She may have crossed the line, but she was still right.

It wasn't Sophie that Peter needed to talk to. It was David, his husband, the man who stuck with him through thick and thin.

Things were difficult, that was true, but it could get better. But first, he had to help himself. And by that, it meant he had to rebuild bridges with those he loved. They could—and would—help him. Sophie was right; they were still there because love was a powerful tool. It was something that he'd urged his own clients to indulge in, in the past, and now it was his turn.

He wasn't cured, not by a long stretch. Like his daughter, Peter knew he had a long journey ahead of him. Peter decided he would take Sophie's advice. He'd talk to David, and to Karen, too. He'd be open and honest, like he'd wished Karen had been during those ghastly early morning hours when they rushed her to hospital.

It was time for him to take control of his life again. Time for him to stop behaving quite so hypocritically. Time to stop letting his demons haunt him on a day-to-day basis. Time to see the light.

Time to just *be*.

Anywhere But Here

"Justin Lawler!"

Justin awoke with a juddering shock. It felt like the whole world had fallen off of his shoulders and he had suddenly been thrown into an entirely different time. An entirely different place. A whole new universe.

Those feelings, he surmised, weren't actually much of a surprise. After all, his whole life had been turned inside out and upside down lately. And then there was Vena... As his thoughts drifted to Parvena, Justin felt his stomach lurch uncomfortably. Part of it was like there were butterflies in his stomach and the rest was a desperate urge to be sick. If only he knew where (and when, and what) she was, then maybe it would be easier. Even so, it didn't change the fact that everything had changed.

"Justin!"

He flinched as the irate English teacher stood at the front of the room, with arms crossed and his right foot tapping impatiently. Justin sighed. If it were fifty years or so ago, the teacher would probably have thrown something hard at his head by now.

Needless to say, he was rather glad that this kind of punishment had been ruled out of schools. Mr McDonough, meanwhile, probably would have preferred a nice trip back to the Good Old Days.

Old McDonough had been a mainstay at the school for far too long. He probably should have retired years ago. At least, that was Justin's view on the matter. Instead, the old boy was still struggling with raucous youths in the Valleys rather than enjoying his twilight years.

Little did the good old English teacher know that it was possible for him to go back to a time when the school rules were simpler. Justin wondered what old McDonough would make of it if he did. He wasn't a scientist, after all. He much preferred to have his nose stuck in a book.

That, Justin could relate to. However, instead of books, Justin preferred to spend his time plucking at the strings of his guitar. Or at least, he had once, before he'd lost it and everything had changed.

Now, he was tired. Too tired. Life had gotten so much more hectic lately. And now, he and Parvena had been separated. He had to save her, but how? Where? And what from?

"Is dissecting the masterpiece that is William Shakespeare's *Hamlet* so below you that you have every right to sleep through my class?"

"No, sir. Sorry, sir," he mumbled and stared down at the notebook in front of him.

Instead of notes on *Hamlet*, it was filled with doodles and sketches. The centaur, with ivy creeping up her body and disappearing into her hair. That fairy who had caused no end of trouble. Parvena's gemstone...

He shouldn't be here. He should be with her. But Parvena had insisted that he go home. That she couldn't put him into danger, not any longer. Justin had argued back; of course he had. She couldn't make decisions for him, but she hadn't listened.

Apparently, he had too many people who cared about him back home. Too many people who would miss him if he died. And a world without Justin Lawler was one that was lacking something very important.

But what about her? Parvena had turned his life inside out and upside down. School, playing football, even messing around on his guitar and trying to make new compositions, it had all been rendered inconsequential and unimportant.

Why would he want to be studying *Hamlet* when he could be exploring what the world, the universe—multiple universes—had to offer?

Parvena had let him in on her biggest secret and then promptly shut him back out of it. Of course it was only natural that he was going to be somewhat morally outraged. How could she expect everything to go back to normal for him after what he'd seen?

And she, she had happily gone to throw herself back into danger. Parvena said she felt morally obliged to help out that damned elf after all the trouble they had inadvertently caused. But although he had wholeheartedly agreed with her, she had shouldered all the blame. She wouldn't let him atone for their sins.

She had just hopped, skipped and jumped right back out of his life.

Their whole time together. Damn it, it was like a flash, a blur. Intense and exciting and deep and meaningful. She was special. She was magic. She had lit the fuse, brightened up his world, made everything go from black and white to Technicolor.

But it didn't change the fact she was gone. How the heck was he meant to even start finding her when he didn't know where to look, never mind having the capability of doing so?

"So, Justin, please tell me. What do Ophelia's actions in this passage tell us about her state of mind?"

He sighed heavily and mumbled some non-committal answer. It seemed enough to satisfy old McDonough and that was enough. The teacher turned to the board and wrote up his answer before turning onto his next prey.

First, he had to get his way through the school day. Living a life that was all over the place was exhausting. He hadn't realised just how difficult it would be to settle back into a normal life, not after everything he'd already seen and done.

And yet, that was exactly what he was expected to do. After all, nobody would believe that he had actually seen a glimpse of the rumbling war between centaurs, elves, and other supposedly mythical creatures and humanity. Albeit, this had happened in a different plane of being, a different universe.

But then, people talked about alternate universes as a hypothesis, not a reality, didn't they? They hadn't seen what was actually out there. They didn't understand the true potential.

He had. Justin knew what was out there. And he also knew that Parvena was potentially throwing herself into grave danger.

"Fine, Lawler. Detention it is, then. Report to me after class," McDonough huffed and moved onto his next target.

Justin rolled his eyes. Knowing old McDonough, he'd probably forget about the detention anyway. It didn't matter. Instead of worrying, Justin picked up a pen and started absent-mindedly doodling. He was meant to be taking notes but what did the works of William Shakespeare have to do with his future? There were more important things to worry about.

Nobody else seemed aware that Parvena wasn't merely away from school because she was sick. Nobody realised he had been away from school for longer than the weekend. If he told anyone, he'd be laughed off the premises.

He needed somebody, anybody, who knew and understood exactly what was going on. Somebody who would realise the truth of these gemstones and the ability to travel between times and universes.

But who? Who could he speak to about it? How could he even begin to think about tracking down Parvena without his own stone?

In truth, there was only one person he knew who he could speak to about Parvena and mysteries of the wider universes.

Her grandfather.

It was better than nothing, a start. The theory was sound. Provided that Parvena's grandfather actually was alive and that he was within this plane of existence, then he could provide the key to finding Parvena.

But then, the thought struck him: how much did he actually know about Parvena? Was she actually native to this universe? Did she really even come from the same planet as him?

As a Drifter, she could stop and stay wherever she wanted. Whenever she got bored, frustrated, or just needed to escape for a while, she could move on.

Of course, Justin had assumed that Parvena was human, albeit from Bangladesh rather than the depths of the Welsh valleys, like him. He'd assumed that she was born within this specific version of Earth, the one he came from, rather than another one.

But, in their few weeks of exhilarating travel, jumping from one experience and universe to the next, he had learned a lot.

Assumptions were a dangerous thing.

Old McDonough, for example, assumed that now Justin was awake, he was actually listening and learning. That he regretted pushing his teacher into giving him a detention. Instead, Justin was sketching and his mind was all over the place. Thoughts about existences and the like were coming thick and fast. Certainly not revelations about Shakespeare's Hamlet and how the issues in it could relate to today.

Justin looked down at the lined paper. What had once been a mindless doodle had turned into ivy, trailing its way up a human torso and into pale blonde hair. The centaur, Divinia.

Oh, how Justin hoped that the centaur and Alfreida, the elf, would keep Parvena safe until he could get her home.

The places they'd visited beforehand: the blue crystalline caves, the trip on the Titanic, witnessing the universe from a Space Station five hundred years in the future, they had all been amazing. But, it was the universe where elves and dwarves and other mythical creatures roamed the woodlands where they stuck.

Perhaps, had they not ran into Alfreida, then maybe Parvena would have come home with him instead.

Justin's head hurt. Too many thoughts were running through his mind, each one forming like a little demon designed to haunt him.

He had to get out of school. He had to find someone to help him. He hoped that he could trace Parvena's grandfather.

He prayed that he would see her again—and soon.

After all, would life even be worth it without her in it anymore?

Justin glanced up at the clock. The second hand seemed to be moving torturously slowly. If he hadn't known otherwise, he'd have sworn it was going backwards.

Soon, soon he would be able to get out of here. And then, he could start trying to trace down this extraordinary girl who had turned his life upside down.

From there? It didn't really matter. Because he'd be with her again and he'd have escaped from the mundanity of this existence. No longer would he have to listen to old

McDonough droning on about Ophelia and Shakespeare and the ilk.

More importantly, he would be with Parvena again. And maybe, just maybe, they could live out the rest of their days, hand in hand, drifting wherever life took them.

His heart skipped a beat. That sounded wonderful.

The Dream Factory

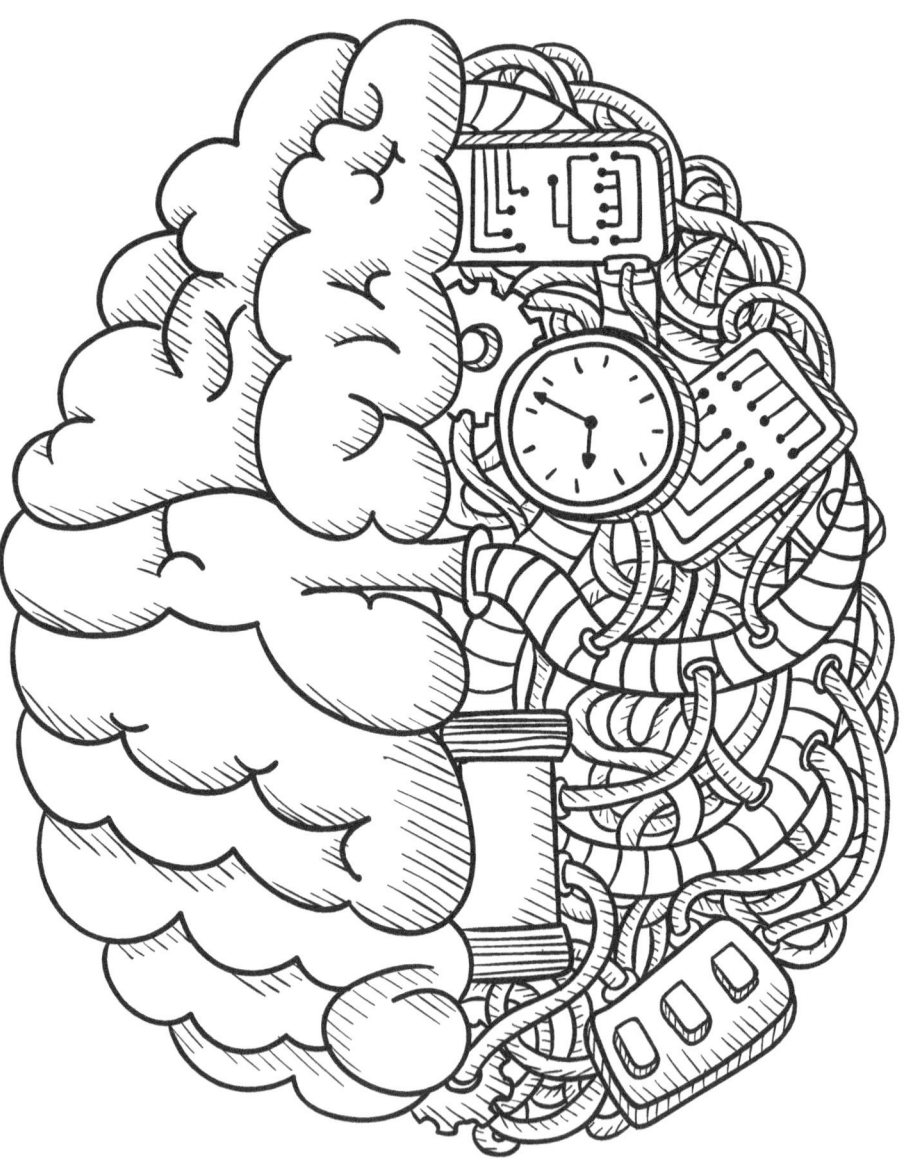

"The brain is a funny place."

The words hung in the air as everybody ground to a sudden halt. It was so quiet that, somewhat stereotypically, you could have heard a pin drop.

Escala swallowed. She had broken the first rule of the factory: you *do not* acknowledge the brain. You never dare break down that wall.

Awkwardly, Escala glanced at her current creation. She was proud of what she had made so far. It was going to be a good one when it was finished.

And yet...and yet, she had allowed her mind to wander. It had traced its way, without her even noticing or being able to acknowledge it, towards the taboo subject.

And of course, she simply had to open her mouth and vocalise it, didn't she?

If only she had actually bothered to keep her mind focused on the task in hand. But then, Escala had always been a bit of a dreamer. She had never learned to focus, to hone her subconscious like the others had.

The silence was deafening. Nobody dared say a word. How could they respond to what Escala had said without implicating themselves alongside her?

Escala, meanwhile, wanted nothing more than to disappear in an instant. However, that would only make things more difficult in the future. She couldn't run away from her problems. Sooner or later, she was going to have to face it.

Minuet appeared beside her, almost as if he had popped up from nowhere. Escala's skin crawled as his aged and wrinkled fingers traced across her shoulders.

"With me," he murmured.

Minuet was the dour sort. With eyes too close together, and bushy, frowning eyebrows, he looked like a perpetually cross grandfather. His moustache matched his eyebrows perfectly. It twitched again and again, like it had a life of its own.

Escala sighed, resigned to her fate. After all, even Minuet's moustache appeared irritated by her unfortunate outburst. Pushing her work to one side, she stood. There was little point in delaying the inevitable.

She winced as her knee cracked. One day, she considered, one day, it would stop doing that. And that day, it would be absolutely beautiful.

They walked down a long corridor. The magnolia walls had black-and-white portraits of previous directors staring sternly down at them. Their imperious gazes made Escala feel a little sick. Her stomach churned. Bile, unbidden, rose up her gullet and into her mouth. She swallowed it back down. It simply wouldn't do to vomit under the gazes of stern directors of old.

There was a brass sign on the bold white door to Minuet's office. His name, engraved in perfect Times New Roman, made it clear that this was his domain. Behind the door, his word might as well have been law.

Escala resisted the temptation to roll her eyes. Minuet always thought far too highly of himself. Of course, he had his eyes on the office just beyond his. In his not-so-humble opinion, it was clear that he believed being the mere secretary to the Dream Director was a position far below his standing.

Sometimes—actually, more often than not, Escala silently corrected herself—he even acted as if there were no higher authority in the factory than he. But then, Escala acknowledged, each one of them deserved their dreams. Even Minuet, no matter how dull, arduous, and repetitive he tended to be.

"After you."

Minuet pushed the door open as he spoke. It moved silently; the joint hadn't even dared to squeak. Lifeless, in Escala's opinion. It was completely lacking in whimsy and charm.

Others, she knew all too well, would have merely believed that it was a sign of a smooth-running operation. She could practically see Minuet spending night after night polishing the frames in the hallway. He would imagine them as being his predecessors, and that somebody else would be diligently looking after his photograph in the future. That was, if the man had any semblance of an imagination at all.

Then, she could see him moving on to oil anything that could possibly creak, whip around with a duster, run the vacuum over the flawless carpets, before finally sitting behind his desk. There, he would await the challenges that were to come. Challenges, Escala believed, that mostly came in the form of her.

She couldn't imagine a life much more dull than Minuet's. She dreamed of dazzling night skies, getting lost in somebody's unfathomable eyes, a cool mountain breeze, the sugar on a doughnut... anything, really, that could make life that little more interesting.

In truth, she could discover delight in just about anything.

But Minuet, he was all about the law and order. Repetition. Perfectionism. How could anyone dream of living up to his exacting standards?

No wonder he craved control. It wasn't surprising he felt stunted and overshadowed by the mere concept of his being simply a secretary. Of course he needed more control.

However, he was a Dream Maker too. That was something they were all expected to do in the factory. But each of them also had other roles to play. Escala knew she was encumbered with communications, but she couldn't say she was especially efficient at it.

It wasn't the first time Escala had found herself somewhat coerced into Minuet's office. She sincerely doubted it would be the last time, either. Even though he was a secretary, he liked to overstep the line and take control of others' tasks if he could. Good job too; she left him to most of the communications as she filled her time in other ways.

Spartan. That was the only way to sum up Minuet's office. Everything was black and white. It was all kept in its place. Everything had a purpose. There was no chance of discovering any little surprises here.

She sucked in a deep breath. She imagined she was inhaling that earthy sweetness of a cat's fur. Calming. Relaxing. Reassuring.

Awkwardly, she perched on the edge of the seat. It was uncomfortable and utilitarian, just like Minuet. He sat opposite her and tried to wipe a speck of dust that didn't even exist off of his right shoulder. Eventually, he steepled his fingers, arched those bushy eyebrows, twitched his moustache, and stared at her.

Escala squirmed underneath the watchful gaze. It felt like Minuet was trying to bore a hole into her, to try and get insight into the very core of her being.

She knew, really, that he was just waiting and watching. Minuet had patience in abundance. He needed it to be able to endure doing exactly the same things all day every day. Changes like her irritated him. But leave him to hypothesise, experiment, and repeat, over and over and over again, and he was content. He'd never lose sight of his goal.

That was too boring. Too much control; not enough wishing, hoping, luck, excitement, daydreaming....

Really, Minuet should perpetually have an ulcer from how much undue stress he put himself under. He needed to learn how to relax, unwind, let fate take the reins, if only for a little while. Everything didn't have to be planned regimentally. It didn't matter if things went slightly awry every once in a while.

After all, that was where things got interesting.

Minuet had grey eyes. Like his silvery hairs, they matched the monochromatic appearance of his office to startling perfection. It was like he was intent on disappearing into the background. Escala swore he was trying to be invisible to the naked eye, but always waiting. Always watching.

She bit her lower lip and scrunched her eyes up as tight as feasibly possible. Her hands were balled into fists, with fingernails digging into the fleshy palms.

She could not—*would not*—break. It wasn't an option.

She shouldn't be here. It wasn't fair. She should have been working on those all-important daydreams.

And yet, she was here. All because of a slip of the tongue.

Escala hadn't meant to say it. The words had just fallen out of her mouth unwittingly.

Besides, what was wrong with them, really? She had only said something that all of them thought every once in a while.

Even Minuet, with his perpetual cleaning, sorting, tidying, monitoring, and overbearing task-mastery, must have had the thought cross his mind every once in a while.

The Director, too.

And really, all she had said was the truth. Albeit in an off-the-cuff, absent-minded type of way. But still, that didn't detract from the fact that it was an accurate statement.

Brains *were* funny places.

So why did she deserve punishment for saying such a thing?

Escala squeezed everything that little bit tighter. She would have given almost anything to get out of here and back to her desk.

Heck, she would have been happy had she been assigned the most mundane tasks within the factory as some sort of punishment. Emptying the bins, picking up litter. Even filing. Because then, Minuet wouldn't be judging her. He wouldn't be waiting for her to incriminate herself further. He wouldn't be planning to send her through another set of double doors to seal her fate.

She wouldn't be living in fear of the judgment of the Director.

At least the Director had the right to scrutinise her, though. She was in charge. Minuet, meanwhile, was a general dogsbody with an inflated ego. He may well have been closer to the Director than the rest of them, but it didn't mean he was actually above them in the pecking order.

Besides, his craftsmanship lacked ingenuity. It was so boring, completely mundane. There was no spark, no imagination. It was just... there.

Escala swallowed again. She couldn't do this. There was too much pressure. She needed to get out of here and fast. She needed the smell of something sweet to raise her spirits. The feel of something soft against her skin to soothe her fraying nerves.

Maybe the Director wouldn't be so bad, after all. She had little to no chance of Minuet understanding her perspective. He was like her polar opposite. He'd never understood her approach, even from the very first day she had stepped through the doors of the factory.

Escala let out a puff of air and blinked furiously. Minuet's expression remained unchanged. His fingers were still steepled. He was still gazing at her over his bulbous nose and bushy moustache. He'd barely moved a muscle in all the time she'd been sitting there.

"Um..." she started.

One eyebrow raised sceptically as Minuet awaited the paltry attempt at an explanation.

"Sir?"

She vaguely realised he hadn't said a word to her since he'd sat opposite her. They'd remained in a silent impasse in this room, the stopping place between the hallways and the Director's office.

But then, that was exactly Minuet's style. Escala had seen it for herself before. He didn't need to ask questions because people would break before him of their own free will. All he had to do was wait.

His long, skeletal fingers unwound themselves from one another and she watched as they tap-tap-tapped against the black desk between Minuet and herself. Each time, it sounded like one of his joints were cracking. *Think of a happy place*, Escala told herself firmly. *Think of a happy place, and then everything will be okay.*

She took in a slow, measured breath, in and out, in and out. She imagined birdcall. Escala could practically see the dappled light between tree branches as the birds tweeted from high up between the rustling leaves.

Escala thought of cats curling around their owners' feet and asking, no, expecting to be fed. Their piteous meows, both pleading and charming, as they headbutted legs and purred furiously. She thought of the urgent, eager barks of dogs as they waited torturously for the lead to be attached to their collar for the most exciting of times. Walking, clearly, was the highlight of their day.

She imagined being amongst them, being one of them. The animals, the owners, a life hidden alongside them. Instead, she was what, exactly? Nobody had taken the time to actually discover and categorise them. They had no true definition.

They worked tirelessly and got no credit for their actions and more than considerable hard work.

Dreams, after all, did not have the decency to create themselves. Somebody had to work hard to craft them. And a good dream was always a work of art, in and of itself. It may not have seemed that way, especially based on some of her colleagues' creations, but it was.

Escala may not have had the focus that some of them did, but she was good at her job. Her dreams were always exceptional and she had every right to be proud.

How could she be punished when her products were so good?

"Escala?"

Minuet's voice had a warning tone to it. There wasn't much unusual in that. His eyebrows were furrowed in irritation. There wasn't anything strange about that either.

Escala would have laughed in his face had she not been in dire straits. She bit her lip again and winced as the sharp pain shot through her body.

This was all because she was still allowing herself to get distracted so easily. But she couldn't help it. It was a part of her nature. Just like Minuet had his eyes on a promotion, she was naturally distractible.

"Escala, I am waiting."

"It, um..." she slurred her speech slightly. Her mouth felt like it had been stuffed with cotton wool. She was under pressure.

"I... I," she stuttered. "It was just a slip of the tongue, sir. I couldn't help it, I...—"

PICK & MIX – T.L.COWELL

Minuet held up a silencing hand and Escala promptly clamped her mouth shut.

"I've heard enough." Any ordinary being—that was, anyone who was not Minuet—would have rolled their eyes at her terrible attempts at an explanation. "In fact, I have heard it all before. From you."

"What... I know but, what are you going to do with me? I... didn't, I don't, the words just come and I couldn't stop myself. And my work is good. I know it is. You do, too. And so does the Director...."

The door behind Minuet slid open just as he was about to retort. Escala glanced upwards. As if she had summoned her, the Director appeared. They had distracted her from her work.

Now, she knew she really was in trouble.

A tall, lithe figure slipped into the monochrome room. Her skin had a honey glow. The suit, perfectly formed but hand-knitted, suited Director Rayna perfectly.

Rayna looked down at Escala. Willowy, but warm, she smiled. Escala would have found it reassuring had she not been in this predicament. Again.

"Escala. I see you're here again."

"I'm sorry, ma'am," she murmured. "I didn't mean to. The words, they—"

"Let me guess, the brain is a funny place?"

Escala stared at the Director, slack-jawed with wide eyes. How could Director Rayna have known the exact words she had blurted out but five minutes ago? Five long, torturous minutes, that felt so much longer than they actually had been.

"Escala, I remember the day that I first started here. I had the exact same thoughts. We all do, from time to time."

Instead of looking at her, Rayna was looking at the wall. She ran her fingers along the frames of Minuet's qualifications. She had a pensive look about her. Tentatively, Escala unclenched her fingers as she watched the Director.

"This is her third infraction this week. This situation must be contained." Minuet sounded irritated, fussy. "Our workers cannot, and will not be capable of producing quality craftsmanship in an environment littered with such self-actualisation."

Rayna narrowed her eyes at Minuet. It was almost as if she had remembered just how annoying and odious the little man could be.

"Minuet, remind me of the standards of this individual's work?"

Of course, she didn't need reminding. At least, that was what Escala believed, based on Rayna's tone.

"Her work is exemplary, but—"

Rayna let out a sigh. Minuet laced his fingers back together and glared at his superior. He wanted to argue back, but didn't quite dare.

The Director, instead, turned her gaze back to Escala. Once again, she smiled warmly. "Keep up the good work."

Escala let out a heavy sigh of relief. From the moment the words had fallen out of her mouth, she had feared the inevitable. Theoretically, Minuet had the power to take steps against her for these infractions. Of course, the decision was ultimately down to the Director, but he could start the process.

"May I go now?" she asked, subdued.

"You may." Escala stood and darted towards the door. "Oh, and Escala?" She ground to a halt upon hearing her name. "Do try and be a little more careful about what you say out loud."

Acknowledgments

Writing a book is like living on a remote island: it can be lonely, it can be scary, and really, you need all the help in the world to make it happen. I'm lucky to have such a wonderful support network behind me in the form of my family, my friends, my writing "team", and of course, my pets.

As a consequence, I would like to thank: Brannigan, Nyssa, Zara, Ajali, Elphie, Athena, Apollo, Rivergrace, Morningstar, Helios, Selene, Takumi, and newest addition, Aurora, for being there for me whether you wanted to be or not. Your quiet wisdom and endless patience means the world to me. Without you, I'd be more frazzled and understand the world and life itself even less than I already do.

However, pets can only get me so far. In reality, I am indebted to the following people for making *Pick & Mix* truly come to life: Elisa Balestri, Tony Bennett, Kim Cowell, Gina Cowell, Stephanie Hood Wittry, Lionel Cowell, and Conny Hempel. Without you guys, this project would have been an absolute financial nonstarter. As much as I enjoy writing, as much as I thrive upon it emotionally, without you, the reality of a book would not happen.

I am also hugely grateful to April Sanders, cover designer, Zara Cowell, cover star cat, T. Morgan, editor, and Mark McKnight, publisher, for all of the hard work you've put in to make this book a project to be proud of.

And one final thank you to you, the reader. Stories only come alive when there's somebody to read it. Thank you.

www.ingramcontent.com/pod-product-compliance
Lightning Source LLC
Chambersburg PA
CBHW070759120626
46557CB00002B/663